# Praise for Shelia Goss

"Goss has an easy, flowing style with her prose."
—*USA TODAY*

"*Hollywood Deception* by Shelia Goss played out like a movie…there was never a dull moment."
—RAWSISTAZ on *Hollywood Deception*

"[This story] grabbed me from the first page…I wasn't able to put it down."
—3RW Online Book Club on *His Invisible Wife*

"*Savannah's Curse* is entertaining until the last second; you won't want to miss a word!"
—Joyfully Reviewed on *Savannah's Curse*

# Look for these titles by Shelia M. Goss

*Now Available:*

*Women in Hollywood*
Secret Relations
Secret Liaisons
Secrets Uncovered

# Secret Relations

*Shelia M. Goss*

Samhain Publishing, Ltd.
11821 Mason Montgomery Road, 4B
Cincinnati, OH 45249
www.samhainpublishing.com

Secret Relations
Copyright © 2015 by Shelia M. Goss
Print ISBN: 978-1-61922-790-3
Digital ISBN: 978-1-61922-737-8

Editing by Latoya Smith
Cover by Angela Waters

This book is a work of fiction. The names, characters, places, and incidents are products of the writer's imagination or have been used fictitiously and are not to be construed as real. Any resemblance to persons, living or dead, actual events, locale or organizations is entirely coincidental.

All Rights Are Reserved. No part of this book may be used or reproduced in any manner whatsoever without written permission, except in the case of brief quotations embodied in critical articles and reviews.

First Samhain Publishing, Ltd. electronic publication: January 2015
First Samhain Publishing, Ltd. print publication: April 2015

# Acknowledgements

I thank God for His grace and mercy. Without Him, none of this would be possible for me.

I can't do a dedication without mentioning my parents who inspired me to be the best I can be: Lloyd (1947-1996) and Exie. To my two brothers, Lloyd F. (Jerry) and John, who I love dearly.

A special shout out to my Goss and Hogan family near and far.

Thanks to my editor, Latoya Smith, for working with me on *Secret Relations* so that it will shine.

A special shout out to Carla J. Curtis, Stacy Deanne, Kandie Delley, Paulara Hawkins, Peggy Love, Michelle McGriff and Mr. and Mrs. Kevin Gill. Thank you all for your words of encouragement during those bleak hours.

Thanks to all that have shown their support to me over the years. I don't have space to list everybody, but here are a few names: Kemmerly Beckham, Sharon "Shaye" Gray, Linda Dominique Grosvenor, Deborah Hartman-Fox, Sheila L. Jackson, Shelia Lipsey, Angelia Menchan, Emma Rodgers, Mrs. Til, Black Pearls Keepin' It Real Book Club, Charlotte Blocker, Gwyneth Bolton, Tina McKinney Brooks, Crystal Brown-Tatum, Jennifer Coissiere, Ella Curry (EDC Creations), Essentially Women, Eleuthera Book Club, Brenda Evans, Pat "Sister Betty" G'orge-Walker, Yolanda Gore, Bettye Griffin, Cynthia Harrison, LaShaunda Hoffman (Shades of Romance Magazine), Lawana Johnson, Troy Johnson, Yolanda Johnson-Bryant, Deatri King-Bey, Kim Knight, J'son Lee, Live, Love, Laugh and Books, Lutishia Lovely, Rhonda McKnight, Alfreda McMillan, Mindful Thinkers Book Club, Darlene Mitchell, Michelle

Monkou, Celeste O'Norfleet, Debra Owsley (Simply Said Reading Accessories), Onika Pascal, Joey Pickney, Farrah Rochon, V Anthony Rivers, Tee C. Royal (RAWS.I.S.T.A.Z.), Brian W. Smith, Olivia Stith, Joyce Swint, Pat Tucker, Tanisha Webb, Tu-Shonda Whitaker, Lutishia Lovely, Vanessa Davis Griggs, Carla Maxie, Erica Vinnett, Shantal Young and all my FaceBook and Twitter friends and the list goes on and on.

If your name wasn't mentioned, it's not that I forgot about you, I just ran out of room. Thank you _____ (fill in your name). I appreciate you all.

**Shelia M. Goss**

# Chapter One

All eyes were on Charlotte Richards' chestnut-brown, oval face as she ended her fifteen- minute speech on the importance of giving back to the community. She'd been the main speaker at the Los Angeles Rebuilding Our Community Charity event where many of the city's politicians as well as celebrities were in attendance. Her speech was spot-on which garnered a standing ovation from those in attendance including his sister, Marie Maxwell, his personal assistant, Priscilla Franklin, and himself.

Charlotte seemed to have a way about her that captured a room. He'd seen her at events before, but tonight she'd mesmerized him to a point where he couldn't keep his eyes off her. The red fitted knee-length dress she wore accented her curves and the diamonds around her neck matched her beautiful sparkling hazel eyes.

"She's beautiful isn't she?" Marie whispered to him after they took their seats.

"Yes, she is." Sean picked up the program and scanned the back of it. "I was looking at her bio. Very impressive."

"You do need a new manager. Why don't you ask around to see what people have to say about her?"

Priscilla cleared her throat. "Are you sure you want another female manager? You know what happened with Dana."

Sean ignored Priscilla and watched Charlotte work the room. "Please. Let's not talk about her right now."

"At least set up a meeting. She could be what you need," Marie said.

Sean thought about it. "I'll check her out."

"I can ask around too," Priscilla said.

Marie turned to Priscilla. "You don't have time. I have a late night flight. I need you to take me to the airport."

"I wish I could convince you to stay," Sean said.

"I've been gone a month. It's time for me to get back to my life in Houston." Sean hugged Marie tight. "I'm going to miss you."

"I'm going to miss you too, but you know you're always welcomed to come visit. Now go handle your business. I'll call you when I land."

Sean said his good-byes and then went to inquire about Charlotte Richards.

Charlotte smiled and took a seat in between her two best friends, Mona Johnson and Kem Phillips. Charlotte met Kem and Mona in college. They all had attended the University of California in Los Angeles. Kem was from Louisiana, Mona from Texas. Since Charlotte was a Los Angeles native she became their tour guide of the city, which later developed into a lifelong friendship. With her busy schedule and high profile job, she valued the relationship she had with Kem and Mona. They'd been through triumphs and tragedies together, one of which being the loss of Charlotte's parents. With her being an only child, Kem and Mona were the closest things to sisters as she could get.

"I don't know if you noticed but you seem to have an admirer," Kem said.

"Who?" Charlotte asked, while picking up a glass of tea and taking a sip.

"Sean Maxwell and don't act like you don't know who he is," Mona responded.

"You should go talk to him. I read somewhere he's looking for a new manager," Kem disclosed.

Charlotte looked around and her eyes locked with Sean's. The tall man with deep dimples and short, black wavy hair walked in their direction. Charlotte felt the heat intensify. She picked up her glass of iced-tea and drank the rest of it in an attempt to cool off.

"Here he comes now," Mona leaned over and whispered.

"He sure knows how to increase the temperature in a room," Kem said.

Charlotte stood to leave the table but she wasn't quick enough. "Mrs. Richards," Sean said, as he towered at least six inches over Charlotte's five-foot-eight-inch frame.

"Mr. Maxwell." Charlotte responded.

"Can I have a minute of your time?" Sean asked.

"A minute...an hour. She has the time," Mona said from in her seat.

Charlotte turned around and mouthed the words, "Stop it." She turned back to face Sean. "Sure. Let's walk."

"I've spoken with a few of your clients and they give you a glowing recommendation. I'm not sure if you've heard, but I'm in the market for a new manager," Sean said in his baritone voice with its slight Southern twang.

"I'd heard something like that," Charlotte responded. By now, they were standing off to the side while others were mingling amongst themselves.

"I would love to meet with you later to discuss the possibilities of hiring your firm."

Charlotte smiled. "Give me a week and I'll have a proposal I think you won't be able to refuse."

Sean reached into his pocket and pulled out a card from his wallet and handed it to her. "This has my address and phone number."

Charlotte held on to the card as if her life depended on it. "I will see you next week."

Charlotte exhaled as she walked back to her table and took a seat.

"Girl, he couldn't keep his eyes off you. He's still watching you," Mona said.

"Really. He *is* hot. But you know my rules. I don't mix business with pleasure," Charlotte stated.

"With Mr. Naughty, I would make an exception," Kem said.

"So I saw him give you a card...are you going to call him?" Mona asked.

Charlotte laughed. "Nothing gets past you, does it? If you must know, he inquired about my business and we are scheduled to discuss the possibilities of

*11*

me being his manager. Nothing more."

"Keep an open mind. He looks like he's interested in more than your managerial skills," Kem said.

"Have you two forgotten what happened with Darryl? After that fiasco I will never date a client. So if I sign Sean Maxwell, it'll be strictly business," Charlotte said.

Mona and Kem looked at each other with eyebrows raised.

"Yea, right!" They said in unison.

# Chapter Two

A week later, sweat dripped down Charlotte's face as she rushed up the walkway to Sean's exquisite two-story house. She was seconds from being late to her ten o'clock appointment. She wouldn't have been late but accidents on the busy Los Angeles 405 San Diego Freeway made the normal rush hour traffic come to a standstill. She paused for a moment in front of the closed door and whipped out her compact mirror and tissue from her purse, wiping her face dry before throwing the items back into her purse. Charlotte reached out to knock on the door just as it opened.

"Mrs. Richards," Sean said.

"It's Ms. Richards." Charlotte shifted her purse on her shoulder and extended her hand.

Sean gripped her hand, the handshake lasting longer than necessary. Charlotte's heart rate increased and she could feel the sweat forming on her forehead. Time stood still as they both stared into each other's eyes until someone from behind Sean cleared his or her throat.

A petite woman dressed in a too-tight mini dress walked around Sean and extended her hand.

"I'm Priscilla Franklin and we're glad you could make it."

Sean added, "Priscilla is my assistant. She'll be helping me make the decision."

"That's fine," Charlotte responded, in a matter-of-fact voice.

A smirk came over Priscilla's face but Charlotte ignored her and focused her attention back on Sean. His voice hypnotized her. Charlotte couldn't help but stare at his full lips. The suit he wore fit him perfectly. She knew it had to be custom made because he had such a broad chest.

"For a minute, I thought you weren't coming and as you know, I'm a busy man," Sean said, as he led her through his home and into his home office.

"You have a beautiful home," Charlotte acknowledged, as he held a chair out for her to sit down.

Priscilla smiled but gritted her teeth as she plopped down in the seat next to Charlotte.

Sean took a seat behind the desk. "Ms. Richards, I've checked out your current and past client lists and I'm impressed."

"Please, call me Charlotte. I hope it means you will consider hiring me as your new manager. As your manager, it will be my job to grow your brand. You have a solid fan base but I don't think you've maximized your earnings potential. My team and I have already come up with several ideas to increase your exposure as well as your financial portfolio." Charlotte retrieved her iPad from her handbag. After opening a file, she handed it to Sean. She jumped a little in her seat. She wondered if he felt the same electric current she felt when their hands brushed against each other during the exchange.

Sean took a minute to review what was on the screen. "This looks good. This is the direction I would love to go in." He placed the iPad in front of Charlotte.

Charlotte eased to the edge of her seat. "I do have one question before we go further. After ten years, why did you decide to change managers?"

Sean's eyes shifted. "Let's just say Dana and I had a difference in opinion on the direction I want my career to go. It's best we parted ways."

Priscilla coughed; one of those fake coughs.

"Do you need to go get some water or something for your irritating cough?" Sean asked.

Charlotte smiled. Priscilla didn't.

"I'll be alright," Priscilla responded.

Sean looked back at Charlotte. "As I was saying, I want to take my career in a different direction. With that being said, after reviewing some of your plans, I think you may be the woman to take me there."

Priscilla coughed again.

Sean looked at Priscilla. " I think you should take the rest of the day off and do something about your cough."

"But..." Priscilla said.

"It'll be paid time off. Go on. I've got a concert coming up and I can't afford to catch your cold. In fact, take the next couple of days off." Sean turned his attention back to Charlotte. "I think I've made up my mind. Charlotte, send my lawyers the papers and it's a deal. Welcome to Team Sean."

Charlotte smiled not only because she got a new client but also at the sight of seeing Priscilla march out of the room upset. Charlotte shouldn't have been gloating about the other woman's misery. Priscilla may actually be getting sick. But Charlotte's own insecurities reared their ugly head. Priscilla was slim and petite compared to Charlotte's taller, more voluptuous frame. Priscilla reminded her of the woman she'd caught her ex-fiancé in the bed with. Darryl was quick to tell Charlotte if she lost weight, he wouldn't have to step outside of their relationship. She'd tolerated Darryl's emotional abuse until the day she caught him sleeping with a woman in the bed they'd shared together.

Charlotte wasn't surprised that Sean surrounded himself with someone who looked like Priscilla. She was sure Priscilla was more than Sean's personal assistant. She probably assisted the chocolate Adonis in sexual ways too. Most of the men she'd been involved with preferred women who looked like Priscilla. Sean was an attractive man with super star status, so she couldn't imagine him not wanting to be with someone who looked as good as he did.

Charlotte had to snap out of it. She shouldn't be thinking of Sean in that manner; especially since he was about to sign a lucrative deal with her management firm.

"Charlotte, are you okay?" Sean asked. "You've been mesmerized with whatever is on your iPad."

Charlotte blushed with embarrassment. "Oh, I was just thinking of an idea

I want to share with you. Not now, but once we get the legal work ironed out."

"You can share it with me, now." Sean's dimples seemed to get wider as the sly grin swept across his face.

Charlotte looked directly into his eyes. "If you must know, I'm concerned about your playboy image. Every time I look online you're pictured with a different woman."

"Who I'm sleeping with shouldn't be anyone's concern." Sean leaned back in his chair.

"You're absolutely correct, however, the companies I plan on pitching ideas to have moral conduct in their contracts and being a playboy isn't a good look."

"Are you sure that's why you're concerned or is there another reason?" A sly grin crossed Sean's face.

"It's strictly business," Charlotte attempted to convince him.

"You can't always believe what you read online." He looked at Charlotte without blinking and said, "I'm a one woman man. When I'm committed, I'm committed. I only need one woman to satisfy my needs and I can reassure you, I will be the only man she needs to satisfy hers."

His voice sent chills down Charlotte's spine. She shifted in her seat, crossed and uncrossed her legs. His eyes seemed to see straight to her soul. If she didn't know any better, she would think he was talking about satisfying her. She really needed to get a grip. She was acting like one of his legion of fans.

Charlotte turned off her iPad and slipped it back in her designer handbag. "If there's nothing else, I think I should be going. I'll have the contract drawn up as soon as possible."

Charlotte stood and Sean did the same. They shook hands across the desk. This time there was no mistaking the magnetic pull but Charlotte chose to fight it. She rushed out the room, down the hallway and out the front door.

Sean didn't need to meet with Charlotte to know he wanted her as his new manager. He'd seen her at various events but after last week's charity dinner he couldn't seem to get her out of his mind. She filled his thoughts during the day and he dreamed of her at night. Most of his friends were into women who were way too skinny; however, he preferred women with a little meat on their bones. Charlotte, with her curvaceous body, definitely fit the bill. He could imagine ravishing every single inch. He watched her walk down the walkway and get into her black Mercedes. *A classy car for a classy woman*, Sean thought to himself.

Sean hated that Charlotte thought he was a playboy. With her being in public relations, she should know better than anyone you couldn't always believe what you read. He was attracted to Charlotte, but not just physically. When they connected the week before, he'd experienced an immediate desire to protect her and heal any of her open wounds. He hadn't felt that way about a woman in far too long, especially with the shallow women he'd come across lately.

Sean needed someone in his life who he could trust and depend on. But he also needed someone who believed and trusted in him, not just his money. His heart was tugging in Charlotte's direction, yet his mind raised red flags. He wasn't sure why but he was determined to find out.

# Chapter Three

A week after Sean and Charlotte's initial exchange, Charlotte took a seat on the cream-colored Italian leather couch in Sean's living room. She held the brown envelope containing his contract in one hand.

Priscilla smiled and without flinching said, "Sean didn't mention you were coming by."

"He didn't know. I decided to surprise him with the good news. Do you know how long he will be on his conference call?" Charlotte asked.

"He should be coming down soon," Priscilla responded.

Charlotte placed the brown envelope next to her on the couch. She pulled out her iPhone and started responding to her emails. She stopped when she felt Priscilla watching her.

Priscilla sat down next to Charlotte. "You know, the only reason he's not with his other manager any more is because their relationship failed."

Charlotte blinked a few times. "Excuse me."

Priscilla looked at the doorway and then back at Charlotte. "You may want to ask him why Dana's not representing him."

"As you already know, I've done that. But anyway, what's it to you?" Charlotte asked.

"I'm just a sister trying to look out for another sister."

Charlotte laughed then placed her phone down. "Oh really. So help a sister out. Educate me on what I don't know since you're dying to get it out."

"Sean and Dana were—"

"Priscilla, I've been looking all over for you," Sean said, wearing jeans and a fitted shirt revealing his muscular biceps. "Did you answer all of the fan mail from my message board?"

"No, but—"

"Then, I suggest you do so. You know I like to get it done at least once a week and today's Thursday," Sean responded.

Priscilla smiled at Sean and got up from the couch. "I'll take care of it right away." She left Sean and Charlotte alone.

Sean said, "Looks like I interrupted something." He took a seat next to Charlotte.

Suddenly the couch seemed too small. Sean's cologne tempted her to get closer, but she eased to the opposite end of the couch instead. "She was telling me about your last manager, Dana."

"What did she say?" he asked.

Charlotte shifted her body so she could be face to face with Sean. "Nothing. Just girl talk. I came over here to bring you your copy of the contract."

Charlotte waved the brown envelope in the air before handing it to Sean.

Sean took the envelope and removed the contract. He looked at the signatures and then placed the contract and envelope on the coffee table in front of them. "You could have had a carrier deliver this."

"I could but I like to provide personal care to my clients when possible," Charlotte said.

Charlotte couldn't admit the truth to him. She used the signed contract to see him again. She wanted to convince herself the attraction she felt for him was a farce. Not only did she prove it not to be true, it only proved to her that the feelings she had for Sean were real and dangerous. Being in close proximity, caused her heart to practically beat out of her chest.

"So what's next?" Sean asked.

Charlotte placed her personal feelings on hold and got back into business mode. "I think we should pursue you getting your own cologne."

"That would be great. I would want one for men and women."

"I've been in contact with a chemist. Now that I have your verbal interest, I will schedule a meeting."

"I'm excited. Aren't you?" Sean said, as he moved closer to Charlotte. Before she could protest he wrapped his arms around her and pulled her into a tight hug. She knew she should let go but she loved the feel of him, his masculine scent all around her. He pulled back slightly and the two stared at each other, inching closer and closer until—

"Sean, your sister, Marie, is on the phone," Priscilla yelled from the doorway.

Sean jumped back and Charlotte sighed with relief. If he'd held on any longer, she knew they'd be kissing right now and kissing Sean wouldn't have been a good idea. If Priscilla hadn't interrupted, their lips would have locked and she would have crossed the line she had no business crossing.

"Go ahead and take the call. We're through here. I need to get back to the office anyway," Charlotte assured Sean. She stood.

"Are you sure? It'll only take a minute," Sean said.

"No, go. Priscilla can see me out," Charlotte assured him.

Sean got up and left the room.

Priscilla said, "Looks like you and I will be working together after all."

Charlotte stood and walked near Priscilla. "We will need to synchronize his schedule so we're all on the same page."

"We can do it now if you like."

Charlotte pulled out a card from her purse and handed it to Priscilla. "Here's my card. Email me his schedule for the next few months and either I or my assistant will be in touch with events we schedule."

Priscilla walked Charlotte to the door. She held the door open and said, "We both want to see Sean succeed, so this relationship should work out for all of us."

Charlotte smiled. "Take care, Priscilla."

Charlotte got in her car and watched Priscilla wave at her from the doorway. She wasn't sure why but she didn't trust the woman. Still, she had to push those feelings aside to do what was best for Sean.

Charlotte pulled off and headed to the office.

# Chapter Four

Charlotte sat at the end of the conference room table staring into space as six of her eight employees left the room. Felicia Holt, her twenty-five year old eager secretary, tapped on the table breaking Charlotte from her trance.

She'd been daydreaming about Sean off and on all day. She needed to push him to the back of her mind because she had a business to run.

"You two can go. I'm alright," Charlotte said.

She looked at Felicia and then at one of her top associates, Jason Lewis. Jason, dressed in an expensive suit, got out of the chair near the end of the table and took a seat closer to her.

"Is there something you want to tell us?" Jason asked.

Felicia fanned herself. "If I'd just come from Sean Maxwell's house I would be walking around in a daze too. He's hot."

"Felicia, how many times have I told you to mind your business?" Charlotte joked, but didn't deny she'd been thinking about Sean.

"My sisters are crazy about him," Jason said. "I personally don't see what all the hype is about."

"He has a sultry, sexy voice. He has a sexy body. He's nice. He's charismatic. He's every woman's dream," Charlotte blurted out.

"Sounds like you know all about him," Jason noted.

"I guess I'll keep my lustful thoughts to myself. I feel like I'd be violating a girl code if I voiced them," Felicia said.

"Felicia, there's nothing going on between Sean and I, so don't even go there."

"I'm just saying," Felicia said.

Linda Marsh, one of Charlotte's employees rushed through the conference room door. She placed her iPad in front of Charlotte. "You need to see this."

Jason and Felicia moved their chairs closer to Charlotte so they too could see what was so important on Linda's iPad.

The headline read: "Dana Reliford, Ex-Manager of R & B Heartthrob Sean Maxwell Found Dead."

"Oh my goodness," Felicia squealed, as her hand went over her mouth.

Jason read out loud, "Police are unsure if it was suicide or foul play. At this time, it's still under investigation."

"I knew you would want to see this since he's one of our newest clients," Linda said.

"Thanks. I'll find out what's going on and let y'all know." Charlotte handed the iPad back to Linda.

"You don't think he had anything to do with it, do you?" Linda asked.

"No, of course not. I'm sure this news came as a shock to him so I'm going to go by and check on him, make sure he doesn't talk to the press. Hold all of my calls," Charlotte said to Felicia as she rushed out of the conference room.

Sean and Priscilla were seated in the living room going over his upcoming tour. The television was on but the sound muted.

Priscilla's phone beeped. She looked down and then up at Sean. "There's an email from Pandora in your inbox. Do you want to respond or do you want me to?"

"What does it say?" Sean asked.

Pandora was an actress and his ex-girlfriend. Their relationship ended when he realized she was only using him to further her career. Over the years, he'd met many women who had ulterior motives.

"She's in town and wants to meet with you," Priscilla said.

"Tell her, I'm busy." Sean didn't hold a grudge against Pandora, but wasn't in the mood to entertain her.

Sean changed the subject and discussed the new venture with Charlotte's management firm with Priscilla.

"I thought you were satisfied with how I've been handling your schedule?" Priscilla asked.

"You're doing great. But Charlotte and her team can take me places you can't."

"I'm not saying you don't need a manager but maybe Charlotte's not the right one."

"If you're worried about your position, you shouldn't be," Sean assured her.

"I'm not. I only meant—"

"Turn it up," Sean said, interrupting Priscilla.

"What?" Priscilla asked.

"The TV. Turn it up. I just saw Dana's name flash across the screen."

Priscilla located the remote and increased the volume. They stared at the television as the news reporter spoke.

"Dana Reliford, known for managing high-profile musicians, was found dead at her Los Angeles home. One of her most famous clients was R & B singer, Sean Maxwell, also known as Mr. Naughty for his sexual lyrics. Police say right now they have no leads or suspects and they aren't sure if Ms. Reliford's death was foul play or suicide. This is Chad Miller, Channel Five news."

Sean's heart dropped as he heard the news of Dana's death. Before he could grasp the news he'd just heard, the doorbell rang.

"I'll get it," Priscilla said, leaving Sean alone.

He stared at the television as the news showed Dana with him and some of her other clients at various events.

"Charlotte's here," Priscilla announced as Charlotte walked around Priscilla and straight to where Sean sat.

She sat down beside him. "How are you doing?" she asked, sounding genuinely concerned.

"I'm shocked. I can't believe it."

Hearing of Dana's death made Sean think of his parents. They were both killed during a home invasion back in Houston, Texas. The only reason him and his older sister, Marie, weren't killed is because Marie woke him and hid them both in a bedroom closet. Otherwise, it would have been their fate too.

Sean thought about Dana's family and the pain they must be going through. "We were no longer on good terms, but I didn't wish anything bad for her," Sean stated with sadness in his eyes. "She was only in her thirties, like us."

"Hopefully, the police will get to the bottom of this and find out what happened," Charlotte tried to assure him. She reached over and squeezed his hand.

Every phone in Sean's house was ringing off the hook. Priscilla could be heard talking in the background as she attempted to answer the calls.

"Do you need me to help filter some calls?" Charlotte asked.

Priscilla shook her head no. "I got this."

Sean couldn't think straight and wondered had he not ended their business relationship would she still be alive.

The doorbell rang snapping him out of his thoughts.

# Chapter Five

Two police officers entered the room behind Priscilla. Sean stood the moment he saw them.

The older officer said, "Sean Maxwell, we're here to ask you a few questions about Dana Reliford. I'm Detective Watkins and this is Detective Mills."

They all shook hands.

"I just heard on the news she'd been found dead," Sean responded. "What happened?"

Detective Mills looked around the room.

Charlotte stood beside Sean. "Sean, maybe you should get your lawyer before answering any questions."

"And you are?" Detective Watkins asked.

Charlotte extended her hand. "I'm Charlotte Richards, Mr. Maxwell's manager."

"Ms. Richards, we only have a few questions. If your client still feels like he needs an attorney afterwards, then by all means, it is within his legal rights to request one," Detective Watkins stated.

"Charlotte, it's okay. Detectives, have a seat," Sean said.

Each of the officers sat in a chair directly across from the couch. Charlotte and Priscilla took a seat on opposite sides of Sean.

Detective Mills pulled out a plastic bag with a piece of paper in it and handed it to Sean. "This was left near Dana Reliford's body."

Sean's eyes scanned the bloodstained letter. He read it aloud, his voice quivering as he did so. "If you're finding this letter, it means I couldn't take living without Sean Maxwell any more. I love him but he doesn't return my feelings. Ending my life like this is only a formality. My life ended the day Sean fired me as his manager. At least with me being his manager, I could be around the man I love. Now, I will be like millions of his fans, only admiring him from a distance. I would rather be dead than live life without him. I tried calling him one last time but he didn't answer and he's not returning any of my calls. It's my sign that it's time to end my misery. Mama and Daddy, I love you both and I'll see you on the other side. To the rest of my family and friends, I love you and will miss you. If by chance, someone runs into Sean, tell him I will love him until the end of time. This is good-bye."

Sean dropped the letter down on the table in front of him. His hands went up to his face as he wiped tears from his eyes. Charlotte reached over, placed her arm around his shoulder, and attempted to comfort him.

He felt more at ease with Charlotte there. Her concern for him touched him in ways she would never know. The only other person he felt genuinely cared about him was his sister. Most of the people who he came across were only nice to him because they wanted something from him. He didn't feel Charlotte fit into that category.

Detective Watkins said, "It appears she committed suicide. Did you and Ms. Reliford have an intimate relationship?"

Sean dropped his head. "She was my manager."

Detective Mills intervened. "We understand, but based on this letter, it seems that Ms. Reliford was in love with you. So again, we ask, were you two intimately involved?"

"No. We never slept together. She wanted more but she knew where we stood. She was my manager and a friend. That's all. I thought Dana understood that."

"Her letter stated you fired her as your manager. Is the sexual relationship the reason you fired her?" Detective Watkins asked.

Sean felt Charlotte's arm drop from his shoulder. "As I just stated, I never had sex with her. I fired Dana because she was not doing her job. I was losing out on gigs or I was late for gigs because she'd become obsessed with me instead of handling my career."

"Sean, I really think you should call your attorney," Charlotte said, between clenched teeth.

"That's all the questions we have at the moment. Right now, it looks like an apparent suicide. But, if after our investigation is complete, we find out it's something else, we'll be in touch," Detective Watkins stated.

Both of the officers stood. Sean walked them to the door. He returned to the living room. Priscilla held a phone up to each ear. Charlotte held her phone in her hand and appeared to be texting someone.

Sean said to Priscilla, "I'm exhausted and I'm sure you are too. Turn the ringers off and take the rest of the day off."

Priscilla ended the phone calls and said, "I got your back. I'm not going to leave you to deal with this by yourself."

"I'm not alone." Sean looked in Charlotte's direction when he spoke.

"I'll order us something to eat and we can sit and reminisce about Dana… you know, the good times," Priscilla said.

"That won't be necessary. Lock up when you leave. I'll see you tomorrow."

Priscilla gave him a tight hug. "Call me if you need me. I don't mind coming back to sit with you."

"I'll be fine," Sean responded.

Priscilla walked out of the room but kept looking back at Sean. Sean moved and turned to face Charlotte, the two staring at each other in silence. Sean had no more words. His emotions were all over the place. He didn't know if he wanted to cry or scream. He sat down beside Charlotte and grabbed her hand. His body felt at ease, as she pulled him into a tight hug.

And he wept.

# Chapter Six

Charlotte knew she should have run the moment the police officers accused Sean of sleeping with his former manager, but the pain she saw in his eyes wouldn't let her. He said he never slept with Dana so she willed herself to believe him. She hoped her arms provided him the comfort he searched for. He gently pulled away and their eyes locked.

Sean leaned towards Charlotte and before she could blink, their lips gravitated towards each other. Charlotte tried to kiss Sean's pain away as their tongues entwined until they both were moaning from desire.

He stopped kissing Charlotte and she felt like she couldn't breathe. She wrapped her arms around his neck and pulled him down to her. Their kisses continued, Sean's hands roaming up and down her body causing her body temperature to rise to a boiling point.

Charlotte threw caution to the wind. It didn't matter he was her client. It didn't matter she barely knew him. At this moment in time, it only mattered that he seemed to need her and she wanted to be the one to comfort him during his time of distress.

Sean paused and asked, "Do you want me to stop?"

"No," Charlotte moaned.

Sean however did stop kissing Charlotte, but only long enough for him to lead her to his bedroom. As soon as they were through the door, he picked Charlotte up and placed her on the king-sized bed filled with fluffy pillows.

Charlotte was impressed at his strength. It turned her on even more. Their eyes locked as Sean gently removed her clothes. He bent down and planted kisses on her neck. Charlotte leaned her head back, closed her eyes and enjoyed the feel of his full, soft lips.

While kissing her neck, he gently rubbed her right nipple, and she couldn't control the moans escaping her mouth. Sean replaced his hand with his lips sending shock waves through Charlotte's body as he sucked on her nipples and used his other hand to explore the rest of her body.

Sean seemed to hit every one of Charlotte's erogenous spots. Part of her wanted to stop him, but she was now at the point of no return. He parted her center with his tongue and his mouth made love to her in a way that had never been done before. Her body shivered as she climaxed in Sean's mouth.

Charlotte's body trembled in delight as Sean eased up from between her legs and removed his clothes. He reached into the drawer next to his bed and removed a condom. She watched as he placed the condom on. She took in the full view of him. He was perfect.

Sean couldn't take his eyes off Charlotte. All he wanted to do was pleasure her and the more she moaned, the more it motivated him. He wanted to imprint his name in her spirit so just the thought of him would make her body shiver. He got on top of her and he felt complete the moment he entered her paradise. He groaned in delight.

He closed his eyes and got lost in a treasure worth far more than money or gold. Charlotte met each one of his thrusts with the same intensity he gave. Sean got lost inside of her and forgot about everything else. Something tugged on his heart the moment their bodies connected.

The room was filled with sounds of their lovemaking and soon, they were both crying out with pleasure as they climaxed together.

Sean gently wiped the hair from Charlotte's forehead, as she lay snuggled in his arms. "I'm really glad you're here," he whispered, unsure if she was awake or had fallen asleep.

He felt her shift in his arms. "Sean, right now you're dealing with a lot. Don't say something you don't mean," Charlotte responded.

"I was only going to say I've enjoyed the time we've spent together. I want to get to know you better and see where this leads."

"Leads? Sean, come on now. We just met. Besides, you're my client. What happened between us shouldn't have happened."

"We're both grown. I knew exactly what I was doing and you did too." Sean felt tension rising in his body.

"It still doesn't make it right," she responded, looking away from him.

"We did nothing wrong."

"I don't normally do this. In fact, do you know how long it's been since I've been with a man?"

Sean placed his finger over her lips. "Shh. I don't want to hear it. What happened between us was beautiful."

"It was, but..."

"No, buts. If I've learned anything from Dana's death it's to not waste any time. I want you and I'm glad it happened."

"I have a reputation to uphold. What will people think if they found out I was sleeping with one of my clients? Especially in light of Dana's death?"

"It's none of their business. Come on, Charlotte. You never would have made love to me the way you did if you didn't feel the connection."

Charlotte got up off the bed and started looking for her clothes. "I got caught up in the moment. I shouldn't have allowed it to go this far."

"Too late. There's no going back to how things were," Sean responded.

"It's unprofessional of me to be sleeping with my client."

"Then assign me to someone else, but, Charlotte, I want you. This wasn't just a one-time thing for me."

Charlotte stared at Sean with a confused look on her face. She looked at the door and then back at Sean. Without saying another word, she left him alone.

His internal voice cried out to her, but no words would come. Her rejection made his heart ache. After losing his parents, it'd been hard to love anyone else besides Marie. Now that he'd found Charlotte, he didn't want to lose her. She was smart, successful and genuinely seemed to care about him. When he heard the front door close, he screamed out in agony at the thought of losing another person he cared about.

# Chapter Seven

It'd been twelve hours and three minutes since Charlotte felt Sean inside of her. As much as she tried to erase the memory of their time together, she couldn't. She'd stopped by the gym to try to get him off her mind but nothing seemed to help. Charlotte increased the speed on the treadmill.

"Slow down or you're going to run right off the machine," Mona said, from the other treadmill.

"She acts like she's running away from something." Kem took a quick sip of water while pedaling on the stationery bike.

Charlotte wiped the sweat from her forehead with the back of her hand. Without looking at either one of them, she responded, "I've got a lot on my mind."

Mona, who was shorter than her two friends and probably the healthiest with her petite and muscular build, stopped the treadmill. She bent down, picked up her bottled mineral water, and took a sip. "Spill it. I haven't seen you this worked up since…well since forever."

Kem, still riding the stationery bike, said, "Not since Darryl."

Charlotte pressed a button to slow down the treadmill. "Can we not bring Darryl into this conversation?"

"So it is about a man?" Kem smiled.

"Yes and no," Charlotte responded.

The mention of Darryl's name brought back bitter memories. Memories that deserved to be dead and buried; especially since Darryl was a former client who almost ruined her career with his lies. When Charlotte got tired of dealing

*Secret Relations*

with his verbal and emotional abuse, she chose to end their engagement. He was used to being the one in control, so when she broke it off with him, he resorted to saying nasty things about her to anyone who would listen. It took her years to rebuild.

Mona tapped her foot. "You might as well tell us now because sooner or later, we will get it out of you."

Charlotte knew keeping things from these two was next to impossible. Out of the three of them, Kem was the most secretive. Charlotte guessed she had to be because she was the producer of one of the highest rated television shows on network TV. She wouldn't even divulge plot twists with them, even after bribing her with a carton of her favorite Rocky Road ice cream.

"You remember Sean Maxwell, right?" Charlotte asked. She slowed down the pace of the treadmill as she talked.

Kem fanned herself. "Of course. I was thinking about writing him into an episode just so I could get an up close and personal look at that body of his."

They all laughed.

"Well, I just signed him on as a client."

"Cool. That makes my job so much easier," Kem said.

Charlotte stopped the treadmill and stood on the floor. "Please promise me you won't say anything to anyone."

Mona and Charlotte were now standing next to Kem on the bike. Mona and Kem looked at each other. They used their fingers and crossed their hearts. Mona spoke out first, "Now spill it."

Charlotte looked around the gym. Although everyone appeared to be in their own little worlds, Charlotte didn't want to take a chance of being overheard.

"I'm going to go change clothes. Why don't I meet you both at the coffee shop on the corner and I promise to tell you everything."

Kem jumped off the bike. "We're going to hold you to it."

Twenty minutes later, the ladies were seated at a table at their favorite hang out spot, a local coffee shop that served some of the finest coffee from around the world and a very relaxing atmosphere.

Charlotte didn't know how to say it so she blurted it out. "I slept with him."

"With Mr. Naughty man himself?" Mona asked.

"Shh. Don't talk so loud."

"Girl, nobody's paying us any attention. They are too busy doing their own thing."

"Mona, you can get a little loud," Kem said.

Mona rolled her eyes at Kem. "This isn't about you. This is about Charlotte finally getting her groove on."

Kem raised her coffee cup in the air. "This calls for a celebration. Your drought is over."

"How long has it been?" Mona asked.

"Five years too long," Kem answered for Charlotte.

Darryl's constant criticism about her weight made Charlotte feel insecure so she'd taken herself out of the dating market. Once she'd lost a few pounds and built her self esteem, dating was no longer a priority, growing her business became her number one priority.

"I'm glad you're getting back out there. You deserve a piece of happiness," Mona said.

Charlotte frowned. "Ladies, this is not good. Sean's a client of mine."

"And?" Mona asked.

"Remember Darryl? Remember how he dragged my name through the mud? It took me awhile to recover from it. No firm would hire me, that's why I started my own."

"What Darryl did was a blessing in disguise. You're your own boss and have quite a few associates working for you," Kem said.

"True, but we all know how quick things can turn. That's why I told Sean what we did last night could never happen again."

Mona tilted her head and asked, "Are you serious?"

"I'm a curvy girl. Do y'all really think I can compete with the models and actresses that want him? No. So why should I set myself up for disappointment and heartbreak."

"Apparently Sean likes your curves, so don't even go there," Mona responded.

Charlotte squirmed in her seat remembering how his lips touched every part of her body.

Kem waved her hand in front of Charlotte's face. "Hello? Earth to Charlotte. Come back," Kem said a few times.

Charlotte's body shook one good time. "Sorry. I zoned out for a moment."

Mona sipped on her hot coffee. Kem did the same. Neither said a word. Charlotte looked from one to the other. "Neither one of you have anything else you want to say?"

Mona shook her head from side to side.

Kem raised her eyebrows. "I wasn't going to say anything, but for a simple booty call, you sure are overreacting."

"There you go. Reading more into it than what's there." Charlotte didn't dare tell them about Sean's confession, not now anyway.

Kem said, "I say do what your heart leads you to do."

"I can't," Charlotte whined.

"If you don't want him, send him my way. I might come in a small package but I have a lot of love to give and something tells me, Mr. Naughty has a lot to give too," Mona muttered.

"I don't think so," Charlotte said, without cracking a smile.

Mona laughed. "Just kidding. I don't want your man."

"He's not my man," Charlotte responded.

"Yet," Kem added. "He's not your man, yet."

# Chapter Eight

Sean finished his daily exercise routine which consisted of sit-ups, pushups and lifting weights. Although Sean could sing, his body was one of the things his female fans found the most attractive about him. He made it a habit to keep in top physical form.

Today, however, his mind wasn't on physical fitness, it was filled with thoughts of Charlotte. The more he thought about her, the more reps he did. He wished she hadn't left the way she did. He tried not to beat himself up for coming on too strong. He really did want to get to know her better. After the way she made love to him, he assumed she would want the same.

A lot of musicians kept an entourage of people around them, but Sean liked to keep his circle small. The smaller his circle, the more control he felt like he had when it concerned his personal information being leaked to the media.

Priscilla cleared her throat breaking him out of his thoughts. She stood in the doorway holding a newspaper. "We need to talk."

Sean set the weights upon the bar and sat up. "Good morning to you, too."

Priscilla frowned. She walked in the room and shoved the newspaper in his hand. "The management firm you hired isn't doing their job. Why is this even in the paper?"

Sean held the paper. He saw a picture of him and his ex-manager, Dana, staring right back at him. The article filled a fourth of the page. He read some of the story out loud. "Sources at the LA police department reveal there is an ongoing investigation. Although the victim left a suicide note, they are not ruling out foul play. Sources revealed that R & B superstar Sean Maxwell has been questioned. More details will follow."

Sean looked up at Priscilla and said, "This isn't too bad. It's the truth."

Priscilla grabbed Sean's hand. "Come with me."

Sean stood and followed Priscilla out of his workout room. She led him to the front of the house. She shifted the curtain so he could see outside.

"What in the world?" he blurted.

At least thirty reporters with cameras and microphones were at the end of his driveway.

Priscilla closed the curtain. "The phone's been ringing off the hook. Every tabloid, news station and blogger wants to talk to you."

"I don't know any more than they know about what happened to Dana."

"So what do you want me to tell everyone?" Priscilla asked.

"Nothing. If we keep quiet, maybe they'll go away."

The doorbell rang. Sean opened the door and a camera flashed in his face. His hand flew up over his eyes. It took him a few seconds to regain his vision. A man in a suit asked, "Sean, can we ask you a few questions?"

Irritated, Sean responded, "No." He then slammed the door.

"Sean, maybe you shouldn't have done that."

"You're right. I shouldn't have answered the door."

"No, I'm talking about slamming the door in the Entertainment News reporter's face. That's not a good look."

"Call Charlotte. Tell her I need to see her ASAP."

Sean stormed off to the bathroom located on the first floor to take a shower. While under the hot water, he moved his head from side to side attempting to release the tension that now resided there due to the media frenzy surrounding Dana's death. Some of the false accusations about the dynamics of his and Dana's relationship filled the news feed.

He blocked out his current situation and allowed his mind to think back on the previous night. Sean felt himself becoming aroused at the memory of making love to Charlotte. Being with her made his world feel complete. His erection deflated when thoughts of Dana crept in.

Sean ended the shower, dried off and placed a robe on. He went upstairs to his bedroom and changed into a pair of jeans and a Lakers jersey.

He went to his home office located on the first floor. Priscilla glanced at him from her desk as soon as he walked in the room. "I talked to Charlotte and she's sending someone over to talk with you."

"That's unacceptable. I thought you understood I wanted to see Charlotte, not one of her associates."

"Don't get all testy with me. I'm only telling you what Charlotte told me."

Sean sat behind his desk and picked up the phone. "What's her number?"

Priscilla got up and walked over to his desk. "I'll dial it for you."

Sean looked at Priscilla. "I got this. What's her number?"

Priscilla recited Charlotte's number and reluctantly went and sat back down. Sean ignored her attitude.

"Charlotte, this is Sean. I need to see you," he said, without any pleasantries.

"Hi, Sean, as I told your assistant, I am sending over Jason Lewis. He's one of my best associates. He will be able to assist you with all of your needs. If for some reason he's unable to, he has been given instructions to contact me."

"But, Charlotte, I really need you."

"Jason should be there shortly. If there's nothing else, I have a conference call I'm late dialing in for. Don't worry, everything will be fine."

Sean stared at the handset. Charlotte hung up on him. If she treated all of her clients the way she was treating him right now, she wouldn't be in business. Sean wasn't used to taking no for an answer. He believed in positive thinking and making things happen. If Charlotte wouldn't come to him, then he would go to her. He grabbed his Lakers hat and headed towards the garage.

Priscilla ran behind him. "Hold up. What do you want me to tell Jason when he comes?"

"Tell him to call his boss. I'm out of here." Sean hopped in his black, fully-loaded Cadillac Escalade and eased out of the garage as cameras flashed.

With all of the chaos going on around him, he needed Charlotte. She was the only one who seemed to bring calmness to his world.

# Chapter Nine

Charlotte felt relieved after working out and having a mid-day break with her friends. But her relaxed mode was soon broken the moment she got Priscilla's phone call. She'd logged on to the internet the minute she got in her office.

Social media exploded with speculation about Sean and Dana's love affair. Some people were theorizing why he could have killed Dana. Charlotte knew how hateful people could be but the things they were saying about Sean were uncalled for. Some of the articles she read were from reputable websites. It was obvious they hadn't checked their sources. Just because Sean wasn't talking to them, didn't mean he was guilty.

Despite her worry for Sean, she'd dispatched Jason to his location because she didn't trust herself around him. She cared about Sean and the mere fact that people were attacking his character upset her. She needed to calm down so she could effectively handle the situation without making it worse.

Felicia knocked on the door and entered her office. She used her notepad to fan herself. "Someone's here to see you."

"I don't have anyone on my calendar. Did you forget to sync our schedules again?"

"No. I will never make that mistake again," Felicia said.

"Who is it?"

"He wanted it to be a surprise but I'll give you a hint. He's fine and did I say hot?" She touched the top of her chest. "And I mean sizzling hot."

Charlotte shrugged her shoulders. "That could be any one of our clients. We do represent some of the best in the entertainment business."

"I'll just send him in. Fix your hair," Felicia ordered, before leaving.

Charlotte didn't think anything was wrong with her hair but glanced in the mirror anyway just in case. She pulled the flyaway over her ear.

Charlotte looked up and her eyes locked with Sean's.

He walked into the room, his earthy cologne filling the space immediately.

"What...what are you doing here?" Charlotte stuttered.

"Since you wouldn't come to me, I had no choice but to come to you."

The closer Sean walked towards Charlotte, the louder her heart beat.

To her surprise, he stopped and sat in the chair in front of her desk.

"But what happened with Jason? He was supposed to call me if you guys had problems. My phone hasn't rung."

"That's because I haven't met Jason yet. He's probably just getting to my place. I left as soon as you and I hung up the phone."

Charlotte tapped her fingers on the desk. "You can't pop up at my office like this."

Sean eased to the edge of his seat. "Am I making you nervous?"

"No...it's just that—"

Sean laughed, a beautiful sound that seemed to fill the room. "I wish I had time to tease you, but I don't. I need you."

"If it's about last night, this is neither the time nor the place to discuss it," Charlotte interrupted.

"If this was about last night, I wouldn't be on this side of the desk. And you would be sitting, but it wouldn't be in that chair but on my—"

"Come on, Sean. Please," Charlotte interrupted him again. She wished she had a glass of ice to cool her off. The thought of riding him like she did last night made her panties moist.

Sean pulled out his iPhone and handed it to Charlotte. "All of those reporters and cameramen are parked outside of my house."

Charlotte scrolled down the page of the website. "I thought this thing with Dana was squashed. Who is this source at the police station leaking stuff?"

"According to TMZ, it's a reliable source and nothing they've said thus far hasn't been true. But people are taking every little bit of information and blowing it all out of proportion," Sean responded.

Charlotte handed Sean back his phone. She picked up her phone and dialed Jason's number. "I know. He's here with me. Head back to the office. Don't talk to any of the reporters."

Charlotte disconnected the call with Jason and put her attention back on Sean. She didn't like the distressed look on his face.

"Some blogger accused me of being a womanizer. That, I'm not," Sean proclaimed.

"I've read the same thing," Charlotte admitted.

"You of all people should know not to believe everything you see or read from the media."

Sean continued to look over things on his phone.

"I don't. Just sharing with you what I read."

Sean looked into her eyes. She stared back.

Neither said anything. The knock on the door broke their silence.

Felicia walked in the room giddily. "Sean, you're the talk of the town. Just got a few calls about you."

Charlotte went straight into PR mode. "Felicia, I want you to type a press release stating Sean will be holding a press conference tomorrow around noon. Since the majority of them have been camping outside of his house, it will be held there."

Sean interrupted her, "I didn't agree to a press conference."

"Do you want my help or not?" Charlotte asked.

"Yes, but…"

"Sean, please let me do my job."

"You do believe me when I said I didn't have relations with Dana, don't you?"

"What I believe doesn't matter. It's my job to make the public believe you're innocent of that act."

"Charlotte, I'm trusting you to help me out of this situation."

"Good. We're on the same page. Jason and I will be over first thing in the morning to prep you."

"I'm a slow learner, so you might want to practice with me tonight." Sean's eyes twinkled.

Even under distress, Sean exuded sex appeal though she could see a bit of sadness in his eyes. Charlotte bit her bottom lip remembering how he made her body feel. She had to snap out of it. She needed to rescue Sean from this media nightmare.

"Sean, I wish I had time to go back and forth with you, but I don't. You need to focus on what's important and right now, it's making sure we deal with what happened to Dana. You'll hear from me later tonight."

Sean stood. "I'm depending on you to get me out of this jam."

"I'm glad you have faith in me." Charlotte felt good knowing in spite of her rejection, he still had faith in her work.

Sean walked towards the door. He stopped and turned around. "For now, we can keep it strictly business. But there will be a time where you'll have to deal with these unresolved emotions."

Sean left without saying another word, leaving Charlotte alone to ponder over what he'd said.

# Chapter Ten

Sean felt a little better after meeting with Charlotte. Knowing she was on his side eased some of the tension. Although Charlotte hadn't come out and confessed her feelings for him, Sean knew within his heart Charlotte cared. The number of reporters camped outside near the curb seemed to have increased since he'd left. He eased his Escalade through the gate barely missing running over a few gung ho reporters who wouldn't move out of his way.

"It's a mad house out there and in here," Priscilla said, as soon as he made it inside of the house.

"I see that. I just came from meeting Charlotte and she's called a press conference for tomorrow."

"I don't think that's a good idea. You haven't seen the other things they are saying about you on the internet. Some people are accusing you of knowing Dana was bi-polar and purposely pushing her over the edge."

"Let them talk. I had no idea of Dana's mental state until she started stalking me. Even then, I didn't know she was bi-polar. I'm not responsible for her death and I refuse to let anyone make me feel guilty about something that had nothing to do with me."

Priscilla stared at Sean. "Please don't repeat that to anyone else because that makes you sound so cold."

Sean took a few deep breaths and walked away from Priscilla. He felt himself getting upset. He walked to the kitchen and poured himself a huge glass of orange juice. He hadn't eaten anything all day so he decided to make himself a sandwich. He sat on the bar stool at the kitchen counter and ate. He turned on the television and started flipping through the channels. He turned it off when he kept coming across coverage about Dana. She wasn't famous prior to her death but now she was on the lips of every news source.

Priscilla walked in with her iPad in one hand and her cell phone up to her ear talking. "Let me find out." Priscilla stopped near him and asked, "When and where is this news conference?"

"Noon and outside near the gate," Sean responded.

Priscilla repeated the information. She placed the phone to her side and asked Sean, "Do you need me to stay the night? I can, if you want me to."

Sean shook his head. "No, not necessary. I have top of the line security. While driving home, I called Trevon with GT Securities and he's going to come by to make sure everything's working right."

The doorbell rang. "That's probably him now."

"I'll check," Priscilla stated.

Priscilla verified who was on the other side of the door as Sean stood nearby.

Priscilla opened the door. A man a few inches shorter than Sean appeared in the doorway. He was dressed in a black suit minus the jacket.

"Come on in," Sean said.

Trevon walked inside. Priscilla cleared her throat. Sean made a quick introduction. "Trevon, this is my assistant, Priscilla. Priscilla, Trevon."

They shook hands. Priscilla smiled and batted her eyes.

"She was just leaving," Sean informed him.

"I could stay." Priscilla looked Trevon up and down.

"I got this. I'll call you if I need you." Sean gave her shoulder a quick reassuring squeeze.

"Bye, Trevon. Hope this won't be the last time I see you," Priscilla said, right before walking out the door.

"You have to excuse her," Sean said. "She can be a little forthright."

"She's not bad on the eyes, but I'm not looking to settle down."

"Priscilla likes to be the one in control so you might want to stay clear of her anyway."

"Hmm. On second thought, I might need to catch up with her. I like to be dominated," Trevon joked.

"T-M-I, my brother."

An hour later, Sean was walking Trevon to the door. Trevon commented, "Everything looks good. Just make sure you start watching the monitors so you can see who is on the outside."

Trevon and Sean said their good-byes. A few minutes later, the doorbell rang. Sean looked at the monitor and saw Charlotte and a man he didn't know standing outside the front door.

Sean opened the door. "Come on in," he said. Sean moved out of their way. He locked the door once they were inside.

"Sean, this is one of my associates, Jason Lewis."

Jason and Sean shook hands. Sean didn't like the fact Jason looked like he could have walked off of the covers of a fashion magazine. He was Sean's height and underneath the tailor-made suit, Sean could tell Jason was fit. Sean tried to keep his jealousy at bay.

"Why don't you two follow me to the den?"

"I would prefer if we held this meeting in your office."

"Sure. You know the way."

Sean allowed Charlotte to lead the way. Jason followed behind her. He noticed Jason checking out his place as they walked. "Nice place," Jason commented.

"Thanks. This is what two point five million will get you," Sean said.

"Nice," Jason repeated himself.

"Would either of you like something to drink?" Sean asked, as Charlotte sat down in one of the plush leather chairs.

Jason sat next to Charlotte while still looking around.

"Nothing for me," Charlotte responded.

"I'm fine for now," Jason answered.

Charlotte removed printed sheets from the portfolio she'd been carrying. She turned the papers around to face Sean.

Sean read over the papers.

"Any questions?" Charlotte asked.

"No questions, just concerns," Sean responded.

"Like what?" Jason asked.

"What if people still want to believe the worse?" Sean asked.

"We can't control that. But you can control how you react and what you say. That's why we're here. To prepare you for that part," Jason responded.

With Charlotte and Jason rallying behind him, Sean felt more at ease for the first time that day.

# Chapter Eleven

Charlotte purposely sat across from Sean so their bodies wouldn't be near one another. The smell of his cologne was affecting her libido. Several times she caught him staring at her with an intensity that made her bite her bottom lip. Thankfully Jason was there to keep them both on track.

"Let's do a mock run," Jason suggested.

Neither Charlotte nor Sean said anything.

Jason tapped Charlotte on the arm.

"Yes, we're going to do a mock run," Charlotte repeated what Jason had just said.

"We'll pretend to be reporters. You relax and answer the questions as best as you can," Jason added.

"What if someone asks me a question, I don't want to answer."

Jason and Charlotte looked at one another. Charlotte spoke out first. "Easy. Say, 'no comment'."

"What if someone asks me a difficult question?"

"We've got you covered. We're going to equip you with an earpiece," Jason said.

"I will be by your side the whole time. Jason will speak into your earpiece if he feels you need assistance answering a question," Charlotte added.

"I'm normally not nervous about these things, but after reading some of the hateful things being said about me, I'm at a loss for words." Sean looked down. The air of confidence he normally showed seemed to have disappeared.

"We're Team Sean and we've got you. There's nothing to worry about.

Right, Charlotte?" Jason asked.

"He's right. Now let's practice."

"Were you and Dana Reliford sexually involved?" Charlotte asked.

"No."

"According to her friends, you two were an item," Jason said.

"I'm not sure of what lie Dana told them, but Dana and I were never more than friends. She was my manager and nothing else."

"Soften your tone a bit. You're coming across as angry," Charlotte pointed out.

"But this is upsetting that I have to defend myself against these false allegations." Sean threw his hand in the air.

Jason said, "It's frustrating, but you have to remain calm throughout. I will let you know when you need to show emotion but it's a sad emotion, not coming from a place of anger."

Charlotte and Jason spent the next hour doing a mock press conference, coaching Sean on how to respond to some of the most difficult questions. Jason raised his hand.

"Jason, put your hand down. This is not school." Charlotte laughed.

"Sean, where's your bathroom? I've held it as long as I can. I'm about to burst."

"We can't have that," Sean responded. He pointed in the direction of the bathroom. "Go down the hall and it's the third door to your right."

"I'll be right back." Jason rushed down the hallway to the bathroom leaving Charlotte and Sean alone.

Charlotte pretended to be reading over the information on the piece of paper in front of her, but she could feel Sean's eyes on her. An electric current ripped through her body the moment his hand touched hers. She jumped in her seat as he squeezed her hand.

"Thank you for helping me out," Sean said.

She avoided eye contact but responded, "I'm just doing my job."

"Do you make house calls for all of your clients?" he asked.

"Yes, sometimes I do." Charlotte wasn't lying. Either she or one of her associates would meet with their clients on movie sets, at home and even sometimes abroad if the situation required it.

Jason reappeared. Sean removed his hand and Charlotte exhaled.

Jason smiled. Charlotte noticed him looking back and forth at her and Sean.

Sean said, "It's late. There's a Chinese restaurant I like to order from. Let me find a menu and call and get something delivered."

Jason yawned. "Nothing for me. I think I'm going to head home."

Charlotte gathered the sheets of paper and began placing them back in the portfolio. "I guess I'll head out too."

Jason shook his head. "No, you stay. I'll pick up something on the way home and I'll see you both in the morning."

"Jason, we came together. How am I supposed to get home? My car's still at the office."

"I have several vehicles or I can call you a cab. Besides, it's a little late. I'm sure your car will be all right. I'll have a cab take you home," Sean offered.

"But..."Charlotte tried to protest, but neither one of the men would let her so she threw her hand up in the air." You both win. I'll stay and have dinner. I want shrimp fried rice and three wings."

"Yes, ma'am. Let me walk Jason to the door then I'll call in our order. Be right back."

Charlotte stood, walked over to the window and peeked through the curtains. She watched Jason get in his car and pull off. The reporters must have called it a night because she didn't see anyone near the gates.

Before she could turn around, she felt an arm around her waist. She closed her eyes and inhaled.

"Sean, I don't think this is a good idea. After I eat, I want you to call me a cab and then I'm going home. In fact, save the food for me for tomorrow. You should probably call me a cab now."

Sean's arms dropped from around her waist. He gently turned her around.

They were now face to face. "Please, don't go. If it wasn't for you, I don't know how I would get through all of this. You have no idea of how alone I feel sometimes," he confessed.

Charlotte felt her heart tug. "You have family and friends."

Sean's eyes darted away. "The only family I have left, that I can depend on is my sister, Marie, and we've already spoken." He shared with Charlotte what happened to his parents.

"Oh no. I lost my parents to a tragedy too. But they weren't shot, they were killed in a car accident," Charlotte responded. Tears filled her eyes.

Sean took one of his hands and wiped the tears from her cheeks. "I didn't mean to make you cry."

Charlotte sniffled. "I'm okay."

"So will you stay?"

"Only if you behave."

"I promise to be on my best behavior." Sean held up two fingers. "Scout's honor."

"Were you a Boy Scout?" Charlotte asked.

"No."

They both laughed.

Charlotte asked, "Sean, are you telling me everything? Is there something more about Dana I should know?"

Sean held Charlotte's hand and looked down into her eyes. "I've told you everything. Dana was my manager and my friend. We were never intimate. I didn't want her in that capacity. It was strictly business between us."

"I hear you," Charlotte responded.

"Please trust me. Can you do it for me?" Sean asked.

Charlotte nodded. "Don't make me regret it."

He kissed the back of her hand. "I'm trying to abide by your wishes but I can't stop thinking about last night. I want you."

Charlotte wanted Sean as much as he wanted her. Her heart pounded. He was so close, she was sure he could hear the sound of her rapid heartbeat.

"I want you too," Charlotte confessed.

Sean bent down and kissed her lips. He eased his tongue inside of her mouth. She didn't resist. Instead, she gasped, as her feet became light. As if sensing she was about to lose her balance, Sean scooped her into his arms and carried her to his desk, sitting her atop of it. He eased Charlotte's skirt up around her waist. He rubbed the outside of her soaked panties before removing them. He threw them to the side of the desk. Charlotte could no longer deny the attraction so she gave in to her feelings. Sean's head dove in between her legs. His soft lips made contact with her lips and he twirled his tongue in and out of her core.

Charlotte leaned her head back, wrapped her legs around his neck, and allowed Sean to pleasure her. The more she moaned, the more tricks he did with his tongue. She tried to control the sensation ripping through her body, but she couldn't. Her legs shivered and she cried out in joy.

# Chapter Twelve

The more Charlotte moaned the more Sean wanted to pleasure her. She tasted sweet and he couldn't get enough of her. "Ooooh, baby, I can't take no more," she moaned.

Sean stopped briefly but only to remove his jeans. He noticed her right leg trembling. The desire he saw in her eyes excited him. He shifted her hips close to the edge of the desk and thrust inside of her.

He moaned in pleasure at the feel of the moisture in between her legs. "Charlotteeee," he said her name over and over.

Charlotte met each one of his moves with one of her own. They rocked back and forth on the desk until they both climaxed. He held her close to his chest until their heavy breathing subsided and seemed as one in a slow even pace.

Sean didn't know what the future held, but he knew at this moment, and at this time, life was perfect. He was exactly where he wanted to be. He didn't just want Charlotte in his life; he needed her mind, body and soul. Being with her completed him and he hoped she felt the same way.

The doorbell rang. Sean hated the delivery guy came as soon as he did. He didn't want to move. The doorbell rang again.

Charlotte said, "The food's here."

"I better go before he starts banging on the door." Sean kissed Charlotte on the lips then put his boxers and jeans back on.

Charlotte eased her skirt down. "I'm going to the bathroom to freshen up."

"Everything you need should be in the cabinets," Sean surmised.

Thirty minutes later, Charlotte and Sean were seated across from each other at the kitchen table eating their Chinese food. Neither seemed to want the night to end as they talked and shared things about their childhood and family with one another.

"I always wished I had a sister. Mona and Kem are the closest things to it. You may not remember them, but they were at the charity event where we met," Charlotte said, right before drinking from her bottled water.

"I'm sure if I see them again, it'll refresh my memory."

"My parents both moved to California from the south so I don't have any family here that I know of. I've basically been on my own since they died."

"I have other family, but Marie's the only family I'm close to. When my parents were killed, we went from house to house. No one wanted the responsibility of taking care of us. Marie lied so she could keep me with her. She pretended to be older than she really was. I don't know how she did it, but she got us housing in the projects. Those were some rough years, but we made it through."

Charlotte reached over and rubbed the top of his hand.

"If your fans only knew the trials and tribulations you've gone through to succeed, they wouldn't dare be turning their backs on you now," Charlotte said.

It touched Sean that Charlotte was concerned.

"I don't talk about it much, but I do talk to the youth and try to encourage them. If a child sees they have hope, then they will try. We have to give our youth a reason to want to do better with their lives."

Charlotte nodded in agreement. "There's more to you that I didn't know."

"There's a lot of stuff you will never read online. If you want to know something about me, all you have to do is ask."

Charlotte pulled her chair closer to the table. "I want to know everything."

Sean went on to tell Charlotte more about his life before becoming a famous R & B singer. "If it wasn't for Priscilla's brother, Dallas, taking a bullet for me, I might not be here today."

Charlotte's mouth dropped open in surprise. "What do you mean?"

Sean's eyes glazed over as he thought back to his late teen years. "I was nineteen years old. I was doing whatever I could to make ends meet. I grew up in the Fifth Ward of Houston. Me and my friend, Dallas, would steal and then resell items to get money. Well, we happened to steal from the wrong person. They wanted to retaliate. Someone identified the car we used. Dallas happened to be in the car by himself and took a bullet. A bullet that was also meant for me."

"I hate to sound selfish but I'm glad you didn't get shot," Charlotte blurted out.

"I sometimes feel guilty that I didn't."

"But, it's not your fault Dallas got killed," Charlotte declared.

"I know but Dallas was like a brother to me. I would have easily exchanged places with him, if I could."

Charlotte squeezed his hand. "So is that why Priscilla's here? You feel some type of obligation to Dallas to take care of his little sister."

"Yes. I promised him I would take care of her and I feel it's the least I could do."

"That's very noble of you. The more I learn about you, the more I'm drawn to you," Charlotte confessed.

Sean smiled. The conversation lightened up and they finished eating.

"The good thing about take out, there's no need to clean the kitchen afterwards," Sean said, as he threw their empty containers away.

Charlotte wiped her mouth with one of the napkins. "This was good."

"Glad you liked it."

Charlotte stood . She glanced at the watch on her arm. "I can't believe it's almost eleven."

"I didn't realize it was so late either."

"You better call a cab for me."

"I have a better idea. Why don't you spend the night?" Sean suggested.

He walked up to her and wrapped his arm around her waist.

She touched his chest. "It's best that I don't. I need to be fresh and well rested for your press conference tomorrow. Not to mention, you do have the paparazzi out front. We don't need another headline."

"I'm not calling a cab," Sean said.

"Then I guess you're taking me home," she responded.

"I guess so. Give me a minute to find my keys."

Fifteen minutes later, they were headed down interstate 405 towards Charlotte's Mediterranean style house. Conversation between them was kept to a minimum. Instead of talking to one another, they listened to some of Sean's latest slow songs. When he reached over to hold Charlotte's hand, she didn't resist.

Once nearing her subdivision, Charlotte gave him directions on how to get to her house.

The houses in Charlotte's subdivision weren't as big as Sean's neighborhood, but they were nice sizes. Charlotte stayed in a three-bedroom brick home with a beautifully manicured lawn and a two-car garage.

Sean heard the barking of a dog when he pulled into the driveway.

"Never mind him. That's my neighbor's dog," Charlotte said, as she unfastened her seatbelt.

Sean went to the passenger door and opened it. "I want to make sure you get in safe and sound."

"You're such a gentleman."

"I'm glad you noticed."

Sean placed his hand in the center of her back as they walked up the sidewalk to the front of her house. She looked inside of her purse.

"You're not going to believe this," she exclaimed.

"What?" Sean asked.

"I left my keys in my desk. I wasn't driving so I placed them in my drawer. I'm screwed."

"Maybe not," Sean said. "I'll be right back."

Charlotte watched Sean as he fumbled in a toolbox he kept in the back of his SUV. He returned holding a crowbar. "Lead me to your back door. Last thing we want is for your neighbors to see me breaking into your house."

"That's one scandal we definitely don't need right now," Charlotte said.

"You're right about that."

Charlotte watched Sean use his tools to open her back door. Her alarm went off and she ran inside to deactivate it.

Charlotte shifted from side to side. "We have a busy day tomorrow. You probably should be going home. I want you to look refreshed for the press conference."

"I will, after this." Sean wrapped his arm around Charlotte and pulled her into a passionate kiss. "Now, I can go."

Charlotte stood there with her lips pouted.

"I'll have a car come pick you up in the morning," Sean said.

Charlotte nodded. Sean heard the latch lock after she closed the door behind him. He wished she would have asked him to stay.

# Chapter Thirteen

Charlotte tossed and turned the whole night. She wished she would've asked him to stay the night. She wanted him to know she cared. Sean made her feel good. Made her feel smart and sexy but she knew with the public allegations hanging over his head, it was best whatever feelings they had for each other be put on hold. She had to get a grip before things spiraled out of control.

There was no need for an alarm because she was awoke before eight. She showered and went to her closet. She pulled out her light blue custom-made power suit. She slicked her freshly relaxed, straight hair back into a high ponytail, did her make-up and then put on her clothes. She accessorized her look with a pair of pearl earrings and a matching pearl necklace. She wore one ring, her birthstone ring, a sapphire on her ring finger of her right hand. Satisfied with her appearance, she slipped into her matching blue Jimmy Choos and waited for her ride to come pick her up.

She didn't have to wait long. A limousine driver arrived minutes later. She checked in with her office while riding to Sean's. Crowds of reporters were already lined up in front of the gate surrounding his home, the limousine easing its way through, to the house. She could see flashes as she made her way up the steps to the front door.

Priscilla's scowl greeted her when the door opened. "Hi, Charmaine."

Charlotte smiled. "I'll give you a pass this time because I realize some people aren't as bright as others. So remembering a simple name like Charlotte may be difficult."

"I'm sorry, Charlotte. I'm a little stressed so please forgive me," Priscilla said as she moved out of the way to allow Charlotte in.

"Sure, no problem. Where's Sean?" Charlotte asked.

"He's in the living room, I think."

The doorbell rang. "That's probably Jason. Send him back if it is." Charlotte walked away in search for Sean.

She stopped in the doorway of the living room and watched Sean for a few seconds before making her presence known. He looked dashing in the black Oscar de le Renta lambswool blazer with a lapel and matching pair of black slacks. He paced back and forth in front of the fireplace.

"You're going to tire yourself out before the news conference," Charlotte said, as she entered the room.

He stopped and looked at her. "I can calm down now that you're here."

Sean walked near her. He reached down to hug her. She didn't resist. She held on to him tight. "It's going to be alright," she assured him.

Neither wanted to let the other go. Charlotte was the first to pull away.

"We need to be careful. Anyone could have walked in on us," she spat.

"But after last night, I thought—"

"We'll talk later. For now, let's table this discussion."

Sean frowned but Charlotte didn't care. Her emotions were all over the place. If she didn't push their situation to the back of her mind, she wouldn't be any good to him today when they went to face the vultures. This was a pivotal moment in his career. She had to push her personal desires aside and do what was best for his career.

Jason entered the room. "Good morning. Is our star ready to face the public?"

Charlotte looked at Sean. "Are you ready?"

"Not really. Maybe you can go out there and speak on my behalf."

Charlotte walked over to Sean. She straightened out the handkerchief at the top of his suit. "You can do this. I'll be by your side the whole time."

Jason walked near Charlotte and handed her an earpiece and a pendant.

"I'm going to clip this pendant right here so Jason can hear what's being asked. Place this in your ear so you can hear him."

"This is a two thousand dollar suit. I don't want a hole in it," Sean said.

"You'll never know it was there. Trust me."

Charlotte slipped the pendant on the pocket with the handkerchief.

"I'm going to test it. Say something," Jason ordered.

"Testing...testing," Charlotte repeated.

"I can hear you. Sean, now we need to make sure you can hear me," Jason said.

They spent the next few minutes testing the audio.

Priscilla walked in. "Sean, I need to see you about something."

"Can it wait? I'm sort of busy right now."

Priscilla frowned, turned around and walked away without saying a word.

Sean asked, "Will y'all excuse me for a minute? Let me go see what's going on with her."

"She needs me to slap her one good time and she'll be alright," Charlotte said, once Sean was out of earshot.

Jason laughed. "I don't think she likes me. But I know she can't stand you."

"I don't think she likes me either. Glad I'm not the only one sensing it," Charlotte responded before glancing at her watch. "It's about show time."

"You got this, boss lady," Jason assured her.

"I've done this many times, but for some reason, today, I'm nervous."

"Maybe because this one is a little personal," Jason noted.

Charlotte ignored Jason's comment. Instead, she said, "It's time to get this show started. Sean needs to hurry up."

"Did I hear my name?" Sean asked as he stepped back in the room.

Charlotte walked away from where Jason stood. "Yes. It's time. Come on."

"We can walk or drive to the end of the driveway," Sean suggested.

"With these heels on, I don't think I'll be able to walk anywhere," Charlotte responded.

"You drive." Sean removed car keys from his pocket and handed them to Charlotte.

Charlotte smiled when she saw the black Maybach sports car in the garage. "I can't wait to see how this baby drives."

Sean didn't know this, but she knew a thing or two about cars. Her father was a master mechanic and before he died, owned his own luxury car dealership. Charlotte knew the sports car had a V12 engine and would love to be behind the wheel to test its speed on the open highway.

A few minutes later, she'd driven them both to the end of the driveway. She parked the car. Sean got out, came to the driver's side, and opened the door for her. He held his hand out to her as she exited.

She wondered if he felt the electric current she did whenever their hands touched.

The sounds of the reporters interrupted her thoughts. She looked at Sean. "Let's do this."

# Chapter Fourteen

Sean tugged on the collar of his shirt. The sweat was irritating his neck. Charlotte's words were reassuring, as they walked to the gate entrance. Reporters were shouting out his name along with questions. Sean couldn't hear what anyone was saying.

Charlotte yelled out, "Quiet please. Sean Maxwell has something he wants to say and then we'll be open for questions."

To Sean's amazement, the reporters stopped talking and a hush fell around him.

Charlotte nudged him.

Sean cleared his throat and looked into the crowd of people. He was glad he wore sunglasses because the flashes from the cameras were a little distracting. He did as Charlotte instructed him the night before. He found one friendly face in the crowd and pretended to be addressing that person while blocking out the others.

He walked to the microphone and said, "I want to send my condolences out to Dana Reliford's family and friends. I know it had to be heartbreaking to lose her in the way they did. I know some of you are here today because you've heard about the police investigation and the suicide note Dana left mentioning her feelings for me. Dana and I had a strictly professional relationship. When our professional relationship ended, I still supported Dana by collaborating with a few of her clients.

"To those that have resorted to saying things about me on social media, I've never intentionally hurt anyone. In fact, I was one of the ones who insisted on

Dana getting medical help when I first noticed her erratic behavior. Unbeknownst to some, she'd been clinically diagnosed as having bi-polar disorder. I'm not a detective or working on her case, so I can only speculate the reason why Dana killed herself is because she was not taking the medication her doctors prescribed for her.

"I'm here talking to you today, not because of what people are saying about me online, but because I don't want Dana Reliford's death to be in vain. I want to bring awareness to mental illness. The results can be deadly...either to the person themselves or those that come in contact with them.

"Since learning of Dana's suicide, I've done my own research. I've decided to donate money to the Mental Health Association here in Los Angeles so that those who need treatment but can't afford it, can get the help they need."

When Sean finished his speech, the reporters raised their hands to get his attention.

An Entertainment News reporter asked, "Is it true Dana Reliford stalked you up until her death?"

Sean took a few deep breaths before responding. "Dana had a lot of issues."

"Why weren't you invited to Dana Reliford's funeral?" Another reporter asked.

Sean looked at the reporter. He heard Jason in his ear saying, "Repeat after me. 'Due to the nature of how Dana died, the family decided on a private ceremony and I respect their decision.'"

Sean repeated what Jason said to him.

A reporter from a local Los Angeles TV station asked, "Some people have resorted to saying mean and hateful things about you online. How do you address your critics?"

"People are entitled to their own opinions. I have no control over that," Sean responded.

Sean answered a few more questions until Charlotte intervened. "Okay, everyone. That's all for today. We thank you for coming. Enjoy the rest of your day."

Charlotte touched Sean on the arm indicating it was time to walk away. Some reporters called out Sean's name as he turned to follow Charlotte to the car, but he ignored them.

Once inside, Sean felt relieved. "How did I do?"

"You did great. I'm impressed. You didn't need my help once."

"Jason helped me with one of the questions."

"You did better than most people. You handled yourself like a pro."

Sounding like JJ from *Good Times*, Sean used his fingers and rubbed his chest. "Well, you know. What can I say?"

They both laughed.

A few minutes later, Sean, Charlotte, Jason and Priscilla were seated in the den watching clippings from the press conference on television.

Sean looked at Charlotte sitting beside him on the sofa. "Thanks to you, everything went well."

Priscilla grunted. "I could have done that."

"But you didn't," Jason pointed out.

Priscilla growled. "I don't like you."

"You're not the first woman who's told me that and probably won't be the last." Jason went back to looking at the television.

Sean shook his head and laughed as he watched the exchange between the two.

Sean said, "I don't know about anyone else, but I'm famished. I was too nervous to eat this morning."

"I'm surprised y'all didn't hear my stomach growling," Jason blurted.

"I haven't had a good hamburger in awhile," Charlotte said.

"Priscilla, take care of it for me, please," Sean insisted.

Priscilla wrote down what everyone wanted and left the room.

For just a second Sean was able to silence the madness around him and enjoy the moment.

# Chapter Fifteen

Charlotte spent the next few weeks making sure she and her team flooded news sources and the internet with positive press releases about Sean. On this particular day, she was sitting behind her desk staring at the blank computer screen. Sean seemed to be depending on her more and more. She was glad he felt like he could trust her but what she didn't want was a repeat of what happened with Darryl.

Darryl got upset with her when he took her advice and it backfired. That's when Darryl started becoming verbally abusive to her and their relationship never recovered from it.

Charlotte didn't want Sean to get mad at her if the press didn't respond the way he'd hoped. She needed to be able to trust Sean's feelings were as real as the ones she felt for him. She needed him to love her not because of what she could do for him career wise, but because he truly loved her, the woman.

She was snapped out of her thoughts when her phone rang. It was Allen Bales, a high school friend of hers.

"How are you stranger? I haven't heard from you lately," Allen acknowledged.

"Not my fault. That wife of yours has been keeping you busy."

"Lily, says hi, by the way."

"Tell her I said hi, too."

"So what's going on with you?" Allen asked.

Allen and she had been friends since high school. She felt at ease opening up to him about her feelings for Sean. "So should I put a stop to it before it goes any further?" Charlotte asked.

"I think you should explore your feelings for each other."

Felicia walked in carrying a huge bouquet of roses. "Look what just got delivered."

"They're beautiful," Charlotte exclaimed as she stood behind her desk. "Allen, let me call you back."

She ended her call with Allen right before Felicia handed Charlotte the two-dozen roses. Felicia held the card from the roses in her hand.

Charlotte smelled the flowers before finding a spot on her desk to place them. "You can give me that," Charlotte said.

"It's from Sean. You must have made a big impression on him. Is there more going on with Mr. Naughty than you're telling?"

"You know I don't mix business with pleasure."

"Come on, you can tell me. I won't tell anyone," Felicia teased.

"Don't you have some more work you need to do?" Charlotte said, chuckling.

Felicia looked at her watch. "It's after six. I'm off the clock. I met the delivery man at the elevator and wanted to make sure you got these."

"Clients send me gifts all of the time so don't read into what's not there."

"I've got my eye on you," Felicia said, as she walked towards the door.

"Bye, Felicia," Charlotte giggled, as she took another sniff of her roses.

Left alone with her thoughts, Charlotte read the note and decided to give Sean a call.

Instead of hearing his sexy baritone, Priscilla answered. "He's busy right now."

"I'm sure he'll want to talk with me."

"Hold on. Let me check."

Charlotte played with the stress reliever ball on her desk while waiting on Sean to get on the phone.

"Hi, sweetheart. Did you like the flowers?" he asked.

"They are beautiful. Thank you," Charlotte responded.

"I've been meaning to give you my other cell number. The one that's for personal use only."

"Good, what is it? Because I'm tired of having to talk to Godzilla's twin sister when I call you."

Sean laughed. "Be nice."

"I'm always nice."

"Sometimes you can be naughty," Sean teased.

Charlotte pretended as if she didn't hear his last comment.

Sean gave her his personal cell number and she entered it into her phone.

"Thanks again, Sean, for the flowers. I have a dinner engagement, so let me get off here so I can freshen up."

"So you're just kicking a brother to the curb?"

"Don't even go there. You're not my only client or have you forgotten that?" Charlotte laughed.

"So I'm just a client to you. I thought I was a little more." Sean sounded disappointed.

"You know you're special to me, so you can stop pouting now," Charlotte said.

"So you're admitting you care?" Sean asked, sounding more cheerful.

"Yes, I care. I've got to go, I'm running late." Without giving Sean time to respond, Charlotte disconnected the call.

After getting off the phone with Sean, she made sure everyone had gone for the day and the office doors were locked. She showered in the bathroom located in her newly renovated office, and changed into a knee length fitted black sequined evening dress. She kept on the pearls she'd worn earlier. The shoes she had on didn't match her dress, so she found an extra pair of black heels in the trunk of her car.

An hour later, she waltzed into the fundraiser for St. Jude Children's Research Hospital held at the Ritz Carlton Hotel. Though the party was live and in full swing, she'd rather be at home on her couch sulking about Sean. But she would never back out of an obligation to the charity.

Mona waved her hand in the air at a table near the door getting Charlotte's attention. She slipped in the chair beside her. She acknowledged everyone at the table, before turning to Mona.

"Sorry, I'm late," Charlotte said.

"Kem called. She won't be able to make it. She sent her assistant here to give me this." Mona held up an envelope. "She sent a sizeable donation."

"Great." Charlotte added the check to her own company's donation in her black handbag sitting on top of the table.

Waiters carrying trays of food walked to each of the tables and started placing meals in front of people.

"I took the liberty of ordering for you, Charlotte. I hope you don't mind."

"As long as it's not salmon, then I'm fine."

A spokesperson for St Jude's Hospital spoke to the crowd while they ate their dinner. After dessert, an announcer walked to the podium and said, "Ladies and gentlemen, we have a special treat. He's been a supporter of our organization and tonight he'll be singing a few songs. Enjoy our entertainment as you mix and mingle with one another."

"I hope it's somebody I like," Mona mumbled.

"I don't care who it is. I'm going to hand over these checks then I'm out of here. It's been a long day for me," Charlotte said.

They left the table and went to the donor's section.

Sean's baritone voice echoed through the venue. After greeting the audience, he began singing one of his popular mid-tempo songs.

Mona whispered near Charlotte's ear. "Your man's here."

"He's not my man."

"Sounds like he's singing that song just for you," Mona teased.

Charlotte turned around and looked in Sean's direction. He stared at her with an intensity that made her heart flutter. The temperature in the room got hotter. She fanned herself with her left hand.

"Whatever. I'm giving the checks and then I'm out." Charlotte handed the jolly woman sitting at the table her donation. She left Mona behind and headed towards the door. Mona caught up with her. "Not so fast."

"I told you I was leaving."

"Not before meeting my new boss. He's a producer and wants to meet you. He's looking for a new manager."

"I'm exhausted. Maybe now isn't the time," Charlotte said.

"These events are for networking. Follow me. I see him standing over there."

As Charlotte looked over at the producer, her heart stopped. He was standing near the stage, forcing her to look at Sean. Their eyes locked and she couldn't look away.

# Chapter Sixteen

Sean could sense Charlotte as soon as he stood on the stage. His feelings were confirmed when he saw her side profile while standing near the donor table. When she turned around, their eyes locked for a brief second.

He wanted to jump off stage to follow her when he noticed her walk towards one of the exits. Luckily, a petite woman rushed over and whatever she said, must have been convincing, because Charlotte was headed his way. The closer she got to him, the wider his smile got as he sang.

His smile faded when he noticed the petite woman introducing Charlotte to a guy. He was her height with perfect, white teeth. Sean felt a twinge of jealousy when the man held Charlotte's hand a little too long.

Sean needed to know who the man was and why the two were exchanging business cards. Get a grip, Sean thought. He was performing. Normally, the stage was the only place he had control but tonight, watching Charlotte and this man was causing him to lose his mind.

Tension eased when the man walked away and started speaking with someone else.

Suddenly, Charlotte looked at him and smiled. All of his previous feelings of jealousy were wiped away. He couldn't understand what it was about Charlotte that affected him, but he couldn't keep his eyes off her. Charlotte and the woman walked back in the direction they came from.

Sean had to do something. He sang, *"Don't go. Please stay awhile. Don't go. Let me show you what I'm all about."*

Charlotte paused as the woman leaned over and said something to her.

They seemed to be in some form of disagreement. Sean continued singing his heart out but sadly, Charlotte kept walking, leaving the other woman who threw her hands up in frustration.

Sean ended his set abruptly. To the audience he said, "Ladies and gentleman, I'm going to take a quick break." He looked back at the band. "The band will entertain you until I return."

The band members continued to play music as Sean exited the stage.

Sean rushed past some of the attendees and tried to make his way towards the door, but too many people kept coming up to him wanting to snap pictures and get his autograph. When he looked up again, Charlotte was gone.

The woman who had been talking to Charlotte walked up to him. "I tried to get her to stay."

"I'm sorry. Were you talking to me?" Sean asked.

The woman extended her hand. "I guess I should introduce myself first. I'm Mona. Charlotte's my best friend."

"Is she coming back?" Sean asked.

"I'm afraid not. She said she was tired and mentioned something about having a long day."

Sean knew he looked disappointed. He began to walk back towards the stage to complete his obligation to the event organizer.

"Don't give up on her. She's been hurt before so treat her like a delicate flower—with care," Mona suggested.

Mona walked away leaving Sean alone with his thoughts wondering about who had hurt Charlotte. Only one other person could give him the answers he needed and she wasn't there. Sean finished his set, hopped into his Maybach and hit the open highway. Instead of going home, he went straight over to Charlotte's.

All of the lights in her house were off except for one. He exited the car, turned on its alarm and headed for the door. He rang the doorbell but there was no answer. He knocked on the door, waited but Charlotte didn't answer. He removed his cell phone from his pocket and was about to call again when the door opened.

"What are you doing here?" Charlotte asked. She stood in the doorway wearing a purple satin robe.

"I would have talked to you at the event, but you left before my set ended."

"It's sort of late and I'm tired."

"I came over to talk," Sean said.

Charlotte removed her hand from near the belt of her robe. It opened slightly revealing her cleavage. "We have to be careful. The last thing we need is for someone to catch us in a compromising position." She bit her bottom lip.

"Look around. No one's here, but us." Sean swooped Charlotte up in his arms and kissed her.

He gently pushed her inside the door and without unlocking their lips, he closed the door and locked the bottom lock with one hand.

Charlotte gently pushed him away. "Whew. You're not giving me a chance to think around here."

"Please stop pushing me away."

Charlotte walked past him, holding onto the belt of her robe. Sean walked behind her. "You can't run from what's inevitable Charlotte."

"Sean, I'm trying to save your career. You were already ridiculed for an alleged affair with your last manager. I don't want to be the cause of another scandal," Charlotte said.

Sean placed his hand on Charlotte's shoulder. She stopped walking. He turned her around. This time, Charlotte didn't retreat. "The Dana situation is bad, but shouldn't interfere with us. I care about you and if you didn't care about me, you wouldn't be concerned."

"I'm not denying I care about you. But you've worked too hard to get where you're at," Charlotte said.

"Let me worry about that," Sean said.

"I don't want you blaming me if it leaked we're sleeping together," Charlotte admitted.

"I would never do that," Sean responded.

"It's happened before."

"What's happened?" Sean asked.

Charlotte looked away. "I made the mistake of getting involved with a client and he turned on me when the advice I gave him backfired. He treated me like dirt and I lost my job over it."

"Baby girl, I'm not him. I would never blame you for doing your job." Sean did his best to try to reassure her.

"It's not just that, Sean," Charlotte eyes darted downward.

"Then what is it? Make me understand."

Charlotte cleared her throat and began telling Sean her story. "I was in my early twenties. One of the major firms hired me straight out of college. All of the trade magazines said I was on a fast track to success. And I was. I was a super star behind the scenes until I met Darryl. You probably know him as Big Boss."

"Big Boss, yes, I know the dude. He rapped on one of my tracks," Sean said.

Charlotte blinked a few times. "I know. That's the only song of yours I don't like."

"So he's the guy who broke your heart and tried to destroy your career?" Sean's forehead crinkled as he attempted to process the information Charlotte shared with him.

"Yes. Big Boss tried to ruin my life. He'd almost succeeded too. When I couldn't help get him out of a legal jam, he turned on me. He started being disrespectful to me. I dealt with it for awhile but after I found him in our bed with another woman, I ended things. I broke off our engagement and that's when he went on a warpath to ruin my reputation. Darryl made me out to be some sex-starved, crazy stalker to anyone who would listen to him. My boss got wind of what he was saying and fired me. They couldn't have someone like me working for them tarnishing their reputation. I had no recourse because I'd signed papers stating I wouldn't engage in any sexual acts with their clients. My reckless behavior got me blackballed. None of the other major firms would hire me."

"That's foul what he did to you, but, sweetheart, you need to let it go. I'm not Darryl and guess what; you're the boss, so you can't get fired."

"That's one of the reasons why I've been so hesitant on moving forward with you."

"Let it go. That's your past. Don't allow what happened with him keep you from receiving love."

Charlotte crossed her arms. "Who are you supposed to be Dr. Phil?"

"I'm Sean Maxwell and I'm falling in love with you."

"I wish you weren't."

"You don't mean that. In fact, you're falling in love with me too and you need to get over your insecurities and admit it." Sean pulled Charlotte closer to him.

Charlotte pouted and then smiled. "Let's get through this situation with Dana and then we can discuss it further. For now, what we have going on has to remain our little secret."

"I'll do anything it takes to be with you. If you want me to keep quiet about us, then I will," Sean responded.

Charlotte untied her bathrobe revealing her naked body. She took Sean's hand and led him down the hall into her bedroom. He stood behind her, pushed the robe down her shoulders, and watched it slide to the floor. He placed kisses along the back of her neck then down the trail of her back.

"Lay down for me, baby," he instructed.

Charlotte did as commanded.

Sean kept his eyes on her naked body while he discarded his clothes revealing his full erection.

"Let me love you," he said, as he eased on the bed on top of her.

# Chapter Seventeen

An electric current flowed through Charlotte's body the moment Sean's lips touched hers. The kisses started slow and increased as the passion they felt took over. The feel of his lips on her neck sent a chill down her spine. One of his hands cupped her full breasts. He stopped kissing her long enough to see the desire in her eyes. He placed one of her round nipples in his mouth licking and sucking while his other hand roamed her body. Sean soon discovered with his fingers how wet she got the more he sucked on her breasts.

Sean placed kisses all over her body. Charlotte moaned in pleasure. She needed to feel Sean inside of her. As if he'd read her mind, he spread her legs open with one of his hands and eased his stiff erection inside of her. She gasped in delight, wrapping her thick thighs around his waist as Sean took them both on a ride of pleasure.

She found herself on the brink of climaxing with each stroke. Sean raised her legs above her head and her muscles gripped him as he deep stroked her. Her muscles spasmed, causing her to have multiple orgasms.

They made love several times throughout the night. Charlotte fell asleep with her head on Sean's chest.

The sunlight streaming through the blinds of her bedroom window woke Charlotte from her sex-filled dream. It had to be a dream. He was too perfect not to be. She dreamed Sean stopped by and they made love throughout the night. When she opened her eyes, Sean's almond shaped eyes were staring back at her. Her dream hadn't been a dream after all.

"I could lay here and watch you sleep all day long," he said, gently brushing the hair from in front of her eyes.

"How long have you been awake?" Charlotte asked, as she tried to gather her thoughts.

"Just a few minutes. Your snoring woke me," he joked.

"I don't snore."

"Yes, you do."

"I don't believe you."

Charlotte liked the fact that Sean stood up to her. Most men were intimidated by her take-charge personality but not Sean. Like last night, it was clear to her that Sean was in full control of her body. Just the memory alone made her wet.

Charlotte eased out of bed. "I can't stay in bed and chat with you all day. I have a business to run."

"So do I. I'm the Sean Maxwell Corporation. I need to start rehearsing for my world wide tour."

"Yes, you do. Jason needs to speak with your road manager to make sure the dates are coordinated."

"I'm sure Jason's on top of things. He seems to be competent."

"He's one of the best," Charlotte responded.

"Good. Now come give me some sugar," Sean said.

Charlotte shook her index finger back and forth. "No can do. I've got morning breath and so do you."

Sean tickled Charlotte. Charlotte couldn't stop laughing. He planted kisses all over her face and on her lips.

Charlotte jumpedoff the bed. "I'll wash your back, if you'll wash mine." She winked at him and headed to the bathroom.

Sean followed behind her.

Her bathroom wasn't as elaborate as Sean's but it was still spacious. She turned the shower on and got inside the stall. She used her finger motioning for Sean to follow suit. He took the soap and towel from her hand and started washing her back. It'd been years since a man had washed her back.

"Turn around so I can see you," Sean commanded.

Charlotte did as instructed. She'd seen Sean's body naked before but with the water droplets on his body, the only word she could think of to describe him was Adonis. Perfect. No blemishes, just smooth and chocolate.

"Don't be shy. You can touch me," Sean said, as he watched her.

She kissed his chest, as her hand roamed his pecs, making her way down his body until she held his erection in her hands. Sean closed his eyes and bit his bottom lip as she used her hand to satisfy him. She replaced her hand with her lips taking him into her mouth inch by inch. He moaned out in pleasure.

After Sean climaxed, they took turns washing each other off. It took them two hours to get dressed. Sean went home and Charlotte headed to her office.

She greeted everyone with a smile before heading to her office. She didn't have time to put down her things when Felicia stormed into the room.

"I know that look. That's a look of a woman who's been thoroughly satisfied," Felicia noted.

Charlotte smiled but wouldn't confirm Felicia's suspicions one way or another. "I'm just trying to get ready for our staff meeting."

"Let me leave you alone to get ready. I'll see you shortly," Felicia said, as she slipped out of Charlotte's office.

Whatever was brewing between she and Sean needed to remain a secret, but it was getting difficult to hide. Charlotte wanted to shout her feelings to the world. Her feelings for Sean were deeper than a mutual attraction. She connected with Sean on every level. She leaned back in her chair and smiled. This feeling she had, she didn't want to end.

# Chapter Eighteen

It had been almost two months since Dana's death. Internet chatter about Sean and his relation to Dana hadn't died down completely, but at least it wasn't the current headliner. Charlotte and Sean got in a routine of seeing each other at least three to four times a week.

Charlotte's job had been keeping her preoccupied lately, but on this particular night, Charlotte agreed to go out with Sean. He insisted on keeping their destination a surprise.

She sat in the passenger side and drifted off to sleep. She felt a light tap on the arm then heard Sean's voice.

"Charlotte, wake up, sleepyhead," Sean said.

"I'm sorry. It's been a long day. Didn't mean to fall asleep on you," Charlotte responded, as she opened her eyes.

Charlotte blinked a few times taking in her surroundings. "Are we at the pier?"

"Yes. I own this yacht and thought we would sail out for tonight?"

Sean got out of the car and opened Charlotte's door. Charlotte followed him onto the yacht. A staff member greeted them upon arrival. Charlotte grabbed one of the flutes filled with champagne from the tray the stewardess offered and sipped on it.

They stood out on deck as the yacht pulled away from the pier and out into the water. The moonlit night acted as a guide.

Charlotte looked up and tried to count the stars but there were too many of them.

"Beautiful, isn't it?" Sean asked.

"Yes, the sky's perfect," Charlotte responded.

"Just like you," Sean said, as he pulled Charlotte into an embrace.

"I wish."

"To me, you are. You have the perfect forehead." Sean placed a kiss on her forehead. "The perfect cheeks." He kissed her on both of her cheeks. "The perfect luscious lips." He kissed her on the lips then used his tongue to gain entry into her mouth.

Charlotte gasped in pleasure. She felt like she was floating on water. She got swept away with emotions as Sean made love to her mouth with his tongue.

Sean stopped kissing her. "Let's go downstairs. I want to show you something."

Charlotte remained silent and followed him.

Sean opened a door. Candles were lit and a full course meal sat on a table with two chairs.

"You're just full of surprises," Charlotte looked at him and said.

After dinner, Sean led her to another room on the yacht. There were rose petals on the floor leading to a bed.

Sean devoured her lips the moment they were behind closed doors. Charlotte felt like she was melting. Both of their clothes were easily discarded and they found themselves naked and on the cabin bed.

Charlotte didn't know if it was the motion from the waves or the fact Sean was inside of her, but either way, she felt a wave of euphoria sweep through her body causing her senses to go into overdrive.

"Seannn," she called out in pleasure as he hit the spot taking her over the edge.

They climaxed together and fell into each other's arms.

A knock on the door the next morning woke them out of their peaceful sleep.

Charlotte gently nudged Sean. "Sean, someone's at the door."

Sean rubbed his eyes. He grabbed his discarded boxers and put them on.

"Coming," he yelled out. He located his pants and put them on. He opened the door and went outside.

Charlotte went to the adjoining bathroom to freshen up. She took the warm towel and washed her face. Staring at herself in the mirror, she noticed a huge passion mark and smiled. Today would be a scarf day.

"Babe, are you alright?" Sean asked from the other side of the door.

"I'm fine," Charlotte yelled back. "Can you hand me my clothes?"

A few minutes later, Sean opened the door with her clothes in hand.

"That was the stewardess alerting me we are back at port. I did inform them we needed to be back on the road by seven so that's why the early morning wake up."

"Give me a minute and then I'll be ready," Charlotte responded.

"Can I watch?" Sean asked.

"Of course," Charlotte teased with a huge grin on her face. She got dressed as they talked.

Sean wrapped his arm around Charlotte's waist from behind. They were now both looking into the mirror. She said, "I chose you because when I look into your eyes I see that you're sincere. I see a man the rest of the world doesn't get a chance to see. I'm fortunate you share that part of you with me."

Sean kissed her on top of her head. He pulled away. "We better go or else, we might be on here another night."

"In that case, come on. We've both got a lot to do today." Charlotte walked out of the bathroom first.

Sean closed his eyes and swayed to the beat, moving his head from side to side. He sang his new single as his band played. *"Something in your eyes tells me... you want me just as much as I want you. Baby, don't fight the feeling. Let me make your dreams come true."*

He'd written the song with Charlotte in mind and it had become a top twenty hit on the Billboard charts.

Sean heard claps coming from the back. Parris Mitchell, an award-winning

R & B singer with a voice some said was better than Whitney Houston's, walked out onstage. Sean stopped singing. They greeted each other with a hug.

Parris said, "You didn't have to stop. You sounded great."

"See you've got a grown man blushing." Sean smiled.

"I'm here. Just let me know what you want me to do."

"I know your time is valuable so we can go ahead and get started. I appreciate you doing the duet with me and agreeing to be here on the opening leg of my tour. That really means a lot to me."

"When Casper played the song to me, I knew I had to sing it with you."

"Let's take it from the top." Sean went to the piano, sat behind it, and started playing.

Parris hummed and then started singing. *"Is it you?"*

Sean responded in song, *"Yes, it's me."*

*"Do you want me?"*

Sean responded, *"Yes. Can I count on you?"*

She responded, *"Yes. Do you feel the way I doooo?"*

He sang, *"Do you love me?"*

*"Yes. Can I trust you?"*

*"Yes. Count on me to forever be true."*

Together they sang the hook, *"Loving you forever is all I want to do."*

They rehearsed the duet until they were both satisfied it was flawless.

Bobby Mack, Sean's road manager, who'd been sitting in the front row of the empty stadium said, "I love the ad-lib you both did at the end. You're going to have the crowds on their feet."

Sean said his good-byes to Parris and continued rehearsing. "Lady," he said, to his female drummer. "And fellas, that's a wrap. We got one more rehearsal and then it's show time."

Sean stayed around after everyone left. He sat behind the keyboards and began playing around with a new song he couldn't get out of his head.

"Sean...Sean," Bobby called out as he walked over to the piano.

Sean looked at him but never stopped playing. "What's on your mind?"

"Twenty cities in thirty days is an aggressive schedule. Just want to make sure you're mentally prepared for this."

"I live for this. I want to be great. I need to be great. I want people to mention my name whenever they think of great singers. I want people to play my songs for years to come. I'm more than ready for this tour."

"I met your new manager. She's cute. A little thick for me, but if she let me, I would hit it," Bobby said.

"Bobby, you will hit anything that will let you. I don't see how your wife puts up with you."

"As long as I keep bringing home those fat checks, she doesn't care."

"Why be married, if you're going to cheat around?" Sean asked. He stopped playing and looked at Bobby.

"I like excitement. I get bored sleeping with the same woman."

"So add a little spice. What if your wife felt the same way you did?"

"Then she and I would be headed to divorce court."

"You better hope she never finds out about your extracurricular activities."

Bobby walked away. Sean never understood men who cheated on their spouses. If he were to ever marry, he planned to be faithful. As far as the sex, he would make sure they kept it spicy in and out of the bedroom.

Bobby better hope while he's out on the road that his wife wasn't having a little fun on the side herself.

Sean went back to working on the new song for his next CD. Since Charlotte insisted they were to keep what was going on between them a secret, he titled the new song, "My Secret Lover."

After he finished working on the song, he left and headed home. He decided to call Charlotte.

"What are you doing?" Sean asked.

"Just working and thinking about you," Charlotte responded.

Sean smiled. "I've been thinking about you too. Can I see you tonight?"

"I really wish I could. I've got a few more things I need to do before I leave. Maybe tomorrow," Charlotte said.

"Call me when you make it home so I won't be worried about you," Sean said.

"I will," Charlotte promised.

"Good-bye, Sweetie."

"Good-bye," Charlotte responded.

Sean decided he would surprise Charlotte with dinner at the office. He got off at the next exit and made a detour in her direction.

# Chapter Nineteen

Sean made it difficult for Charlotte to keep her distance. She had to find a way to push her own selfish needs and desires to the side until the Dana situation blew over.

It was getting late and she had paperwork to finish. Everyone had left the office. She forgot to check the locks on the front door. She got up to check and almost stumbled when Sean walked in carrying a takeout bag.

"I figured you could use something to eat since you're still here working."

"I could, but I thought you were on your way home."

Sean smiled. "I wanted to see you. Correction. I needed to see you." He glanced back. "It's not safe for you to be sitting in here with the doors unlocked."

"I was on my way to lock them," Charlotte said as they both stood there looking at each other.

Sean asked, "Is there somewhere else we can go to eat or do you want me to put the bag on your desk?"

"Let's use a conference room."

"After you." Sean moved out of Charlotte's way.

Charlotte could feel the intensity of Sean's eyes on her back as she led them to one of the conference room. "We can eat in here."

Sean removed the plastic containers from the bag. "I brought us some Chinese food. I hope you don't mind."

"Does it look like I turn down a meal?" Charlotte sat down across from Sean.

"All of your weight is in all the right places. Men like me love to have something to hold on to."

Charlotte responded, "I rarely see a woman my size in any of your videos."

"Then we will have to change that. Maybe you can star in my next one."

"I don't think so. I'm not a video vixen."

Charlotte began to feel a little self conscious about her size. She was slightly overweight, but fit. She was toned and most of her fat was in her breasts and butt. She decided to change the subject. "How's rehearsal?"

Sean shared with her how rehearsal went over dinner. "It took a minute for me to get into the groove of things but once I pushed the situation with Dana to the back of my mind, I was able to do what needed to be done."

"Good. That's what you need to do. Concentrate on your music. Eventually, things will die down and the media will be talking about something else."

Charlotte loved how passionate Sean was about his work. From their conversation and from the videos she'd watched prior to taking him on as a client, she knew he put a lot into his performance. "I'm proud of you," Charlotte said. "Glad to be on this journey with you. Your first tour where you're the headliner."

"I can't wait for the tour stop in Houston. I've got some special things planned for that trip."

"Do tell," Charlotte said, as she took her last bite.

"You'll have to come to find out."

"I might just do that."

"I also want you there next week when the tour opens up here."

"I wouldn't miss it for the world."

"You have a VIP all access pass and if anyone gives you any problems, you get in contact with me," Sean said.

"Oh. I won't have any problems. You forget. I'm Charlotte Richards. Manager to the stars. I will get in. One way...or another."

"Glad you're on my side." Sean laughed.

"I'm glad you feel that way, Sean. It's important to me that you know I'm on your team. I support you but I have to keep my distance when we're in public."

Sean leaned back in his chair and crossed his arms. "Why?"

"Sean, you know why. If you're not going to think about your career, at least one of us has to."

Sean pulled out his cell phone and then handed it to her. "Look at this."

Charlotte stared at a picture of them standing side by side outside his gates at the press conference. "Why are you showing me this?"

"We look damn good together. When I'm going through a crisis, you're the woman I want by my side. I wouldn't be able to get through this mess with Dana if it hadn't been for you."

"Jason helped too."

"Yes, sure he did, but you're the woman who spearheaded it. You took a bad situation and turned it around for me and possibly brought awareness to mental disorders in the process."

"You make it sound like I'm a saint."

Sean reached across the table and held the tips of her fingers. "To me, you are. You are that and so much more."

"You always know what to say." Charlotte blushed. "I have a few more things I need to do so I need to get back to work."

"Go. I've got this." Sean said, as he looked at the empty containers on the table.

Charlotte smiled before placing a soft, slow sensuous kiss on his lips. She squeezed Sean's hand then got up and left the room.

# Chapter Twenty

Sean cleaned the conference room. He dumped the empty containers and bag in the trash can and walked to Charlotte's office. Her door was shut. He placed his hand on the doorknob to turn it but at the last second, he didn't. He sat down on the leather love seat in the waiting area. It was late and he didn't want her leaving the office by herself. He played around on his cell phone until he heard the clicking of her heels coming down the hallway.

She jumped a little when she rounded the corner and saw him sitting there. "When you didn't come to my office, I assumed you were gone."

"I would never leave without saying bye," Sean said. He stood and placed the cell phone in his pocket.

Charlotte dangled her keys out in front of her. "Let me lock the doors,"

"I'll wait for you by the elevator," Sean responded.

They rode the elevator down to the parking garage in silence. There were only a few cars left.

Their cars were parked by each other. Sean walked to Charlotte's door. She deactivated her alarm. He held her door open while she got inside. "I'm speaking at the Fight for Cancer dinner. Would you like to go as my date?" Sean asked.

"Us, being seen in public as a couple is not a good idea, right now. I thought you understood that," Charlotte responded.

Sean looked her directly in the eye. "Remember, you were my first choice. Since you're turning me down, I guess I'll have to ask Monet."

"Monet, the model?" Charlotte asked.

"One in the same. Besides, she's been having her people reach out to me for a while. If she's available, might as well. The woman I want to go with doesn't want to be seen with me."

Charlotte gritted her teeth. "Sean, you're not being fair. While you're out having fun, I'll be doing my thing. In fact, since it's a charity dinner, I might see about buying a ticket myself. Yes. That's what I'll do."

"Suit yourself. I guess I'll see you Saturday night," Sean responded. He saw the flash of jealousy in her eyes. He knew he was playing with fire, but if it took him being with another woman to get Charlotte to stop worrying about what others thought, then so be it.

---

Charlotte ran her hand across the bottom of her brand new dress.

"You better be glad I'm a married man because, sister, you are wearing the hell out of that dress," Allen said, as he held open his car door for her to exit.

"This old thing," Charlotte joked. "I'm glad you like it. I normally don't wear red."

"I don't see why not. Your friend is definitely going to notice you tonight."

"I didn't wear this dress for him," Charlotte responded.

"Sure, you didn't," Allen smiled, as he held out his arm.

Charlotte placed her hand on top of his arm as he led her up the stairs to the doors of the five star hotel.

They were escorted inside and Charlotte saw several people in the entertainment field as she and Allen made their way to the banquet hall.

"Don't look now, but there's Sean Maxwell," Allen leaned down and whispered.

When Charlotte saw Sean standing there in his black tuxedo next to Monet, the green-eyed jealousy monster reared its ugly head. Charlotte hated she wasn't the one on Sean's arm. If she hadn't been concerned about keeping their relationship a secret, it would be her and not Monet.

It didn't help that Monet was wearing a sheer black dress that seemed to draw attention to every one of her curves. Charlotte started feeling self-conscious about choosing to wear the low cut, yet elegant red dress she wore.

"Come on. Let's go find our seats," Charlotte said, grabbing Allen's hand.

Sean wanted to know who the man was sitting with Charlotte. He would soon find out because he made sure he and Charlotte would be seated at the same table.

"Hi, Charlotte," Sean said, when he and Monet reached the table.

Charlotte mumbled, "Hi, Sean."

Sean looked so good in his suit that she found it hard to keep her composure.

Sean held out the chair for Monet. "This is Monet. I don't know if you two have had the pleasure of meeting."

Monet turned her nose up in the air. "No, we haven't," Monet said.

"Nice meeting you, Monet." Charlotte plastered on a fake smile. On the inside, she secretly wished Monet would disappear.

"Likewise," Monet responded.

The man seated next to Charlotte cleared his throat. "I'm Allen. A good friend of Charlotte's."

"How good of a friend?" Sean asked, as he sat down next to Monet and directly across from Charlotte.

"Very good," Charlotte responded, while looking at Allen.

Sean frowned. "Well, any friend of Charlotte's is a friend of mine."

Allen said, "It's nice to finally meet you. I've heard so much about you."

"I hope they were all good things."

Before Allen could respond, Charlotte intervened. "Allen, I think I left my phone in your car. Do you mind checking for me?"

Allen didn't hesitate to do so.

Monet pulled out her compact mirror to look at her reflection. "Sean, I hate to do this to you, but I see someone I really must talk to. I want to be in this movie and he's just the man who can get me the role. I'll be right back."

Monet leaned down and kissed Sean on the cheek. Sean smiled. He looked and Charlotte wasn't smiling at all.

"Jealous, are we?" Sean stated, glad he was making Charlotte uncomfortable.

"I have nothing to be jealous of," Charlotte responded.

"You got that right, because, baby, if we were by ourselves, I would rip that dress right off your body."

Sean could see Charlotte blushing. "Shh. Someone might hear you."

"Like I care. And why did you bring your boy toy with you tonight?"

"Allen is not my boy toy. He's a good friend of mine."

Sean leaned down on the table. "And I ask again. How good of a friend?"

"Now who's the one jealous?" Charlotte stared back at Sean with a huge grin on her face.

Sean smiled. "Maybe, I should just find him and ask him."

Sean left Charlotte seated at the table by herself.

# Chapter Twenty-One

He wouldn't. Charlotte kept saying to herself repeatedly. She sat at the table waiting for Allen or Sean to return. Monet slipped back into her seat.

"I see our men have disappeared on us," Monet commented.

"It appears that way," Charlotte responded.

Monet said, "Look. I can tell something's going on between you and Sean, so we might as well cut to the chase."

Charlotte's heart dropped. She hoped she could convince Monet otherwise. "With me and Sean, it's strictly business."

Monet laughed. "Please. The sexual tension between you two is so thick, not even I could stand in between it. I'm only here with Mr. Naughty because I knew there were going to be some Hollywood executives here. He's yours."

"Who said I want him?" Charlotte asked.

"Honey, your eyes, your mouth and your body are crying out for him."

Charlotte felt exposed. She couldn't believe her feelings were so transparent. She had to get a grip of herself. "You're reading more into it. Nothing's between us."

"Honey, you can deny it all you want to, but I know the truth."

Before Charlotte could say anything else, Allen and Sean approached their table.

"Did you miss me?" Sean asked, looking directly at Charlotte.

Monet responded, "We sure did. Didn't we, Charlotte?"

Charlotte cleared her throat. "It was quiet with the two of you gone."

Allen chuckled. "Charlotte, no need to have an attitude."

Charlotte looked at Allen. "I thought you were my friend."

"I am. That's why I did what I did."

Charlotte's eyes widened. "What did you do?"

"Nothing. We'll talk about it later," Allen responded, as the waiters came to place food and drinks on their table.

Charlotte couldn't enjoy the meal. She found herself looking across the table at Sean. Sean kept his eyes glued on Charlotte as Monet seemed to dominate the conversation.

"Sean, I hate to leave you, but I just got a text from my agent. I'm needed in Paris tomorrow and if I don't leave now, I'll miss my flight," Monet said.

"I'm scheduled to speak next, so I can't leave, but I will call a cab for you," Sean responded.

Allen said, "No need to do so. Monet, I'll take you home if Sean can make sure Charlotte gets home."

Charlotte listened to the exchange.

"Problem solved." Monet slid her chair from behind the table. "Charlotte, nice meeting you. I'm sure we'll meet again." Monet looked down at Sean. "Don't be a stranger."

Without another word, Monet and Allen left the two of them alone at the table.

"Well, I'm up next. Can I count on you to cheer me on?" Sean asked, while a wicked grin spread across his face.

Charlotte's eyes twinkled.

Suddenly, she heard the announcer's voice. "We would like to thank Sean Maxwell for the outpouring support he's had for our charity over the years. Without further ado, let's give a hearty welcome to R & B legend, Sean Maxwell."

Everyone clapped. Sean looked at Charlotte before pulling away from the table. She gave him a reassuring smile.

Sean was used to performing in front of sold out arenas but standing in front of people in a setting like this always made him nervous. The fifteen minutes he was talking seemed more like fifteen hours to him. He received a standing ovation at the end of his speech. He stopped and talked to several people as he made his way back to his table. To his dismay, Charlotte wasn't there.

"I bet you thought I left, didn't you?" Charlotte said, as she snuck up on him.

Sean sighed. "I sure did. So how did I do?"

"You were great, but you didn't need me to tell you that," Charlotte responded, as they stood there.

"Charlotte, hearing it come from you, means a lot."

"Well, I can call a cab so you don't have to worry about seeing me home."

"No. I'm a man of my word. I will be dropping you off as soon as this event is over."

The announcer came on the loud speaker. "The dance floor is now open." The music blasted throughout the room.

"Would you do me the honor?" Sean extended his hand out.

"Might as well put this red dress to use," Charlotte said, as she followed Sean to the dance floor.

They spent the next twenty minutes dancing and enjoying each other's company.

Sean pulled out Charlotte's seat. "Glad to see you're enjoying yourself."

"I'm glad I stayed," she responded, as she motioned for the waiter's attention.

"May I help you?" the waiter asked.

"Yes. Can I have a glass of Chardonnay?" Charlotte asked.

"Anything for you, sir?" the waiter asked, looking in Sean's direction.

"I'll have the same," Sean responded.

Soon, they were so caught up in conversation, they weren't paying much attention to everyone else in the room. Sean had so many things he wanted to say but didn't want to spoil the mood.

"It's been a long week. I hate to be a party pooper, but I'm a little tired," Charlotte said.

"We can leave. Let me have my driver meet us out front." Sean removed his cell phone from his pocket and sent a text message to his driver.

"Sean, there you are," one of the female organizers said. "Can I get you to take a quick picture?"

"You caught me just in time. I was just about to leave."

"Great. It'll only take a minute."

Sean looked at Charlotte. "I'll be right back."

"I'll meet you out front," Charlotte responded.

Twenty minutes later, Sean and Charlotte were seated in the back of the limousine.

Sean wondered what was going through Charlotte's mind. She remained quiet during the trip to her house. He wanted to hold her, but refrained from doing so. The driver pulled up in front of her house.

Sean got out, went to the other side, and held her door open.

Charlotte took his hand and exited the back of the limousine.

"Thank you for the ride home."

"It's my pleasure."

Charlotte began walking, Sean behind her.

"You don't have to walk me to the door," Charlotte said.

"I want to make sure you get in safe and secure," Sean replied.

"Suit yourself." Charlotte continued to walk up the driveway.

When she reached the front door she fumbled in her purse for her keys.

"I hope you find your keys. We don't want a repeat of the last time. I don't have my tools on me." Sean laughed.

Charlotte dangled the keys out in front of her. "I'm prepared tonight." She opened the front door and turned around to face him but blocked him from entering. "You have a interview at five on the morning show so you need to go home so you can get some rest."

"Not without doing this first," Sean said.

Sean pulled Charlotte into a loving embrace and kissed her passionately.

Charlotte was the first to pull away. "Good night, Sean."

Sean waited for her to walk inside. Once he heard her lock the door, he walked back to the limousine. Although he wanted to stay, Charlotte was right. If he didn't go home and get some rest, he would wake up with bags under his eyes and he had to be rested for his interview.

# Chapter Twenty-Two

Sean intensified his morning workout. He needed to release some of the frustration he felt. Charlotte's need to keep their relationship a secret was beginning to take its toll on him. It upset him when he first saw Allen with Charlotte. He felt some relief when he discovered Allen truly was just one of her friends. Sweat dripped from his forehead as he sparred with the boxing bag in front of him. He punched the bag over and over.

"Somebody must have pissed you off, the way you're hitting that bag," Priscilla blurted, walking in wearing a short white mini skirt and low cut lime green blouse holding her iPad.

Sean stopped briefly. He picked up a nearby towel and wiped the sweat from his face and neck. "It's Sunday. What are you doing here?"

"Your tour starts this week so there were a few things I needed to do today like finalize your schedule and follow up with a few people." Priscilla walked near him and looked him up and down. "Your fans will appreciate how hard you work out."

"I do it for the ladies." Sean went and grabbed a bottle of water from the mini refrigerator and drank it.

"I have a question about the after party. Who do you want on the list?"

"The usual people," Sean responded. "Oh and don't forget Charlotte and Jason."

"Will do."

"Be sure you spell her name correctly, two t's, because I don't want there to be any problems," Sean said.

"C-h-a-r-l-o-t-t-e, I know how to spell her name."

"Good. Just want to make sure there are no misunderstandings."

"Sean, I wasn't going to say anything, but I don't want to see you ruin your career over some woman."

Sean sat down on his weight bench. "What are you talking about?" Sean sounded irritated.

"I care about what happens to you. I don't want to see you get hurt."

"Besides this Dana situation, all is well in my world, "Sean stated.

"It could get worse if you keep messing around with Charlotte. She used to date the rapper Big Boss and he said she tried to ruin his career. You can look it up. It's all over the internet." Priscilla tapped on her iPhone. She then placed it in front of Sean.

Sean moved it out of his way. "I don't need to see it. I know all about Darryl and his lies." Sean leaned back on the bench and lifted the weights up and down. "This conversation is over."

"But, Sean—"

Sean started counting his lifts out loud, ignoring Priscilla.

Priscilla finally seemed to get the point and left him alone. He stopped when she was out of earshot. He placed the weights on the bar then sat up.

He located his cell phone, and dialed Charlotte's number. He got her voicemail. "Charlotte, I really need to see you. I'll be over around four."

Charlotte's plan to lounge around the house alone got interrupted. Someone repeatedly held down the doorbell. Wearing a jogging suit and a scarf around her head, she got up from the sofa and went to the door.

She looked through the window first and then opened the door. "Sean, what's wrong?"

Sean, dressed in a pair of jeans and a t-shirt, stood holding several grocery bags in the doorway. "I left a message informing you I would be coming," he said.

He walked inside without waiting to be invited in.

"My phone's on silent. I didn't want to be disturbed." Charlotte closed the door. "The way you were ringing the doorbell, I thought something bad had happened."

"I'm going to cook for you," Sean boasted. "Direct me to the kitchen."

"Hold up. You don't just come in someone else's house and tell them what you're going to do. For all you know I've already eaten," she snapped.

"Have you?" Sean asked.

"No, but that's not the point."

Sean ignored Charlotte's rant and walked through the house with Charlotte on his heels.

"Where's your seasoning? I forgot to get some when I was at the store," Sean said, as he placed the bags on the counter.

"I haven't given you permission to use my kitchen, yet."

"I don't need it. I'm here now so I'm going to cook. Whether you like it or not." Sean removed the items out of the bags and placed them on the counter.

"Sean, you better be glad I'm not in the mood to argue." Charlotte frowned.

"Neither am I. Do you mind getting me a big boiler, a skillet and a long pan?" Sean seemed unmoved by the fact that Charlotte was frustrated.

Charlotte retrieved the items he requested and made plenty of noise by slamming the cabinet doors as she removed them. She placed the items on top of the stove. "Anything else?" she asked.

"No. I've got it from here," Sean said.

Relieved that Sean's visit wasn't business-related but now she wondered what could be wrong. Charlotte left Sean in the kitchen alone. She went straight to the bathroom to jazz up her appearance. She removed the scarf from her head and pulled her hair back into a ponytail. She brushed the wand from the tube of lip-gloss across her puckered lips. She exchanged her jogging suit for a pair of jeans and a purple Laker's t-shirt. Satisfied with her appearance, she headed back to the kitchen to see what had Sean frazzled.

# Chapter Twenty-Three

Charlotte re-entered the kitchen. Sean smiled when he looked at her. "You're so beautiful."

"Thanks. You have it smelling so good in here," Charlotte said, as she admired the dishes he'd prepared.

"Dinner will be ready in about ten more minutes. Go have a seat and I'll bring your plate to you."

Charlotte left the room as Sean removed the garlic bread out of the stove. He cut it into several slices. He placed some on each one of the plates. He carried the plates to the dining area and sat one in front of Charlotte and the other in the chair across from her.

"Shrimp fettuccine Alfredo. I hope you like it," he said.

"One of my favorite dishes," Charlotte responded.

"I'll be right back. I forgot the wine." Sean walked back to the kitchen and returned holding a bottle of wine and two wine glasses.

He removed the cork from the bottle and poured each one of them a glass. He then took a seat across from Charlotte.

Sean held his wine glass in the air. "To us."

"To us." Charlotte tapped his glass with hers. She placed the drink on the table, picked up her fork and began eating. "Umm. This is good," she said.

"Glad you like it."

"I'm impressed. I didn't know you could cook like this," Charlotte praised, in between bites.

"I've always loved to cook. I like experimenting and trying new things. If I didn't make it as a singer, I would have become a chef."

They ate dinner with hardly any other words between them. Sean washed down his food with another glass of wine.

Charlotte stood and grabbed their empty plates.

"I've got this."

"My mom always taught me if someone else cooks, you can at least do the dishes," Charlotte said.

"Who am I to argue with that? I love to cook, but I do hate doing dishes," Sean confessed.

"I'll wash. You dry," Charlotte instructed.

Sean removed the empty wine bottle and wine glasses from the table and followed Charlotte into the kitchen.

They chatted while Charlotte washed dishes. "Are you ready for Thursday night?" Charlotte asked.

"I think so."

"Do I hear some doubt in your voice?"

"Promise me you'll be there," Sean pleaded.

"I told you I would be."

"I'm going to hold you to it," Sean promised.

Charlotte went back to washing dishes. Sean made sure their hands touched when she passed him the last dish.

He took the dish from her and laid it on the counter before devouring her mouth with his. Sounds of pleasure could be heard throughout the kitchen Sean took one of his hands and stopped her from unbuckling his pants. He pulled away. "Before we go any further, we need to talk."

Charlotte seemed to be in a daze. "I thought this is what you wanted."

"I want more than just sex from you. I want a commitment. I want to know that you're mine and you can be reassured I'm yours. The next time we make love, I want you to savor the moment and let yourself go. I don't want you holding back because you're so concerned with what other folks think."

Sean walked away. He went to her living room and took a seat on the couch.

Charlotte sat next to him. "Sean, I feel great after we make love. If it wasn't for our circumstances, I would shout from the roof top how I felt about you. But I live in reality and I know the outcome. I don't want our personal relationship to cause more problems for you."

"I'm not Darryl. I'm able to separate our personal relationship from business." Sean looked at Charlotte hoping she could see the pain in his eyes.

"You just don't understand." Charlotte looked away.

"Then help me understand. Make me see the fact that you're denying yourself and me a chance of happiness. I know we could be great together."

"We are together. Isn't what we have good?"

Sean clenched his teeth in frustration. Charlotte was being stubborn. He needed her to understand he wanted her and didn't care who knew about it.

Charlotte felt like the walls were closing in on her. She was falling in love with Sean without a doubt but she couldn't risk having their relationship go public. If something drastic happened, she didn't think their relationship nor her reputation would be able to survive it.

"You're everything a woman wants in a man. You're sensitive to my needs. You're caring and compassionate."

"Then why, Charlotte? Why won't you give in to your feelings and let's start building a life together?"

Charlotte looked away. "Let's let things die down first and then we can talk about commitments and going public."

"Dana should be a non-factor in this. I can't keep putting my life on hold because of what happened to her." Sean's tone sounded harsh to Charlotte.

"I can't believe how insensitive you're sounding right now, Sean."

Sean's eyes pleaded with Charlotte. "I hate what happened to Dana. I really do, but why am I having to pay for something I had nothing to do with?"

"It's only temporary. Give it another month or two and then we can decide."

"If you can't give me a commitment then maybe we should reconsider everything," Sean said.

"So what are you saying?" Charlotte stared at Sean. She didn't like ultimatums.

"It's all or nothing, Charlotte."

"Why can't you just accept things the way they are?" Charlotte asked.

Sean dropped Charlotte's hand. Her reasons for not making a full commitment didn't sit well with him. "Good-bye, Charlotte."

Sean stood and walked to the front door.

Charlotte walked behind him. "Don't leave like this. Nothing has to change."

"Things already have." Sean didn't bother to look back as he walked out the door and got into his SUV. He hit the steering wheel before he pulled out of the driveway and roamed the streets of Los Angeles to clear his head.

# Chapter Twenty-Four

After the gym, Charlotte recanted what happened with Sean the night before to Mona and Kem over coffee at their favorite little spot.

"Sean wouldn't have to beg me for a commitment," Mona proclaimed.

"How long are you going to allow Darryl to control your life? He's still winning. You've given him power that he shouldn't have," Kem added.

Charlotte looked at Kem. "I know you're not trying to school me. You can't talk. You're still holding a grudge over your dad about something that happened twenty years ago."

"That's different. He abandoned my mom when she needed him. You and this Darryl thing should be over. But you keep holding on to it. It's wreaking havoc in your life," Kem surmised.

"For the last time I'm over Darryl. I'm trying to do the right thing. The police are still investigating Dana's death and with the public scrutiny surrounding it, I don't want to cause Sean any more problems."

Mona fanned herself. "Girl, forget the public. You got to live your life. Go call your man and make things right. If you don't, some other woman will come along and snatch him up."

After talking with Mona and Kem, Charlotte drove back home, changed her clothes and headed to the office.

Felicia greeted her with a smile. "Parris Mitchell's in your office. I hope you don't mind me telling her she can wait there."

"No. I forgot she was coming in this morning. Can you hold my calls, please?"

Charlotte walked inside of her office. Parris turned around and said, "I was just admiring your pictures on the wall."

"Sorry, I'm late. I worked out this morning and thought I had enough time to make it for our meeting."

"No problem."

"Have a seat," Charlotte said, as she walked around and sat behind her desk.

Parris sat down. "You come highly recommended."

"Thanks. But I'm curious. Carmen Cain's your manager and she's one of the best in the field. Why are you seeking my services?"

Parris eased to the edge of her seat. "It's not public knowledge yet, but Carmen's retiring. She's met a man and they're getting married at the end of the year. She's moving to Florida."

"Wow. I can't believe she's giving up her agency because of some man."

"Love will do it to you. But it's not just because of her future husband. She shared with me she'd been a workaholic for years and up until she met Franklin, her company was her husband."

"As women, we should be able to have both." Charlotte tapped her foot under the desk.

"I agree. I think she's just tired of it all and wanted a change."

"I need to give her a call. She's one of the few people who stood by me during that fiasco of mine a few years back."

"Carmen says you remind her of herself when she was your age. She has a lot of respect for you."

"I'm honored to know she feels that way."

"So, are you going to be my new manager or not?"

"I'll be in touch with Carmen and we'll make it happen." Charlotte extended out her hand to Parris. "Welcome to the family."

"Thank you."

Charlotte grabbed a business card and handed it to Parris. "This has all of my contact information, including my personal cell phone number. Don't hesitate to use it."

"I won't."

"I'm glad America's sweetheart will now be on my roster," Charlotte said. "Come. Let me introduce you to some of the associates."

Charlotte took her around the office. "This is Jason. He doesn't know it yet, but he'll be the one managing you."

Jason moved from behind his desk and shook Parris' hand. "Wow. No words."

Parris looked at Jason and then at Charlotte. Charlotte said, "Excuse Jason. He's not normally at a loss for words."

"I apologize. I've been admiring your work for years. To be able to work with you is a dream come true for me," Jason explained.

Parris smiled. "I'm glad you feel that way, Jason."

Charlotte led Paris out of the room. "Jason's been with me since the beginning. He's good at what he does. You won't be disappointed. He's good with details and when he needs to be stern, he can be."

"I can sometimes be bossy so I hope he's ready for me," Parris responded.

They finally circled back to the lobby. "Parris, this is the end of the tour. I'll contact Carmen's office. You should be receiving a contract within the next few days."

Charlotte watched Parris leave and smiled knowing that with Parris on board, the possibilities for expansion were endless. She stopped by Felicia's desk.

"I need you to schedule a meeting with Carmen Cain for me. The sooner the better."

"AM or PM?" Felicia asked.

"Whatever time fits her schedule. If it conflicts with something else, rearrange those other appointments. This meeting is very important. If it goes the way I want it to, we might be expanding around here."

Felicia smiled. "Does this mean I get a raise?"

"Who knows? You just might." Charlotte smiled.

"I'll let you know what she says," Felicia said.

Charlotte went to her office and closed the door. She sat behind her desk, leaned back in her chair and closed her eyes. She needed to figure out what to do about Sean. Her friends' words hadn't been lost on her. She wanted to be with him and knew if she didn't act now she could lose him forever. Why did things have to be so complicated?

# Chapter Twenty-Five

The days leading up to the opening of Sean's tour kept him busy. It hurt him to walk away from Charlotte like he did but he wanted a full commitment from her. Maybe time apart would give her time to think and make her realize what they had was worth it. She didn't need to be concerned about what others thought. She only had to trust him enough to be there regardless. Sean just didn't have the strength to convince her of that right now. He had to focus on his upcoming tour. He needed to give his fans what they deserved and that was an exhilarating performance.

Bobby came to Sean's dressing room. "It's almost show time. The performer before you is about to end her last song."

Sean looked at him, "I'm watching the screen. I'm ready."

Priscilla walked in behind Bobby. "Sean, all of the guests you personally invited are here."

"Good. I want you to have the president of my Fan club escorted back here after the show. Where's the gift bag I told you to get for her?"

"It's hidden behind the curtain." Priscilla pointed.

"Great. Well, I need a minute alone. The show's about to start."

Priscilla left the dressing room. He heard the door open again. "I told you I needed some time alone," he said, before looking up.

"I'm sorry. I knocked. I guess you didn't hear me," Charlotte responded.

Sean's eyes admired the sequined top she wore with a pair of black fitted jeans that accented her thick thighs and behind. Her hair that she normally kept in an up do was curly and cascading down her back.

"Charlotte. You came."

"I try not to break my promises."

Neither moved closer to the other. "The show's about to start."

"I know. I just wanted you to know I was here. I'm going to go back to my seat now."

Charlotte left him alone. Sean wanted to cry out in frustration. She kept sending him mixed signals. She wouldn't give him the commitment he wanted, but here she was acting like a supportive girlfriend.

Bobby stuck his head in the door. "It's time, Mr. Naughty."

Sean shook thoughts of Charlotte out of his head. He said a quick prayer and left the dressing room. He smiled and spoke to the crew in the hallway as he made his way towards the stage.

The announcer said over the loud speaker, "Ladies, are you ready? I said, ladies, are you ready… to be taken to the *Love Zone?*"

The crowd screamed.

Sean closed his eyes and listened.

The announcer continued, "Sean, I handled the foreplay, you just give them the climax."

The crowd screamed louder. Sean stepped out on the stage. "LA, how y'all doing out there?"

He heard various responses being yelled from the sold out stadium.

He repeated himself. "I said, LA, how y'all doing out there?"

More screams could be heard.

Sean started singing an up-tempo song. *"If your man won't act right, call me. I can do what he won't do. I can make your body sing a new tune."*

The background singers sang, *"Call me."*

Sean sang several songs, the audience getting wilder with each performance. "This song goes out to all the lovers in the house." The band started playing softly. Parris Mitchell walked on stage in a white satin pants suit trimmed with gold and sparkling diamonds.

Sean yelled, "Ladies and gentleman. Parris."

The crowd screamed. Parris walked to the center of the stage. Sean sat behind the piano in a corner of the stage. Together they sang the duet, "Loving You Forever."

At the end of the song, Sean moved from the piano to join Parris as they faced each other and sang in unison. *"Loving you forever is all I want to do."*

Sean kissed Parris on the cheek. He held up her hand and she took a bow.

"Parris, everyone," Sean said.

Parris blew out kisses at the fans and walked off the stage.

Sean walked back to the piano. "I think we're going to keep it at this level. I wrote this song while thinking about a special lady."

Sean sang a few more songs. He now stood at the edge of the stage. Two male dancers who were shirtless danced behind him.

With the mid-tempo beat playing, he sang, *"Can I make your body sweat?"*

He walked off the stage and down in front of the open space in front of the audience with security near him.

*"Can I make your body sweat?"* Sean repeated himself. He touched women's hands in the audience as he walked by. They screamed.

*"It's just you and me, girl. Let me make your toes curl,"* Sean sang. One woman wouldn't let go of his hand, but he had to pull away so he could walk to the other side of the stage to show his fans in that area some attention.

One of his security guards handed him a rose and he gave it to a fan.

"I love you, Sean," she screamed out.

"I love you too." He then went back to singing the song. He handed out several more roses while security followed him.

He jumped back on stage.

"Thank you, LA," Sean said, before taking his final bow and exiting the stage.

# Chapter Twenty-Six

Charlotte, with Jason fast on her heels, attempted to make her way through the crowd of people backstage. Everyone wanted to get close to Sean. She attempted to get his attention, but there were too many people. He never looked her way.

Jason grabbed her arm. "Come on, Charlotte. We'll catch him at the after party."

An hour later, the limousine with Charlotte and Jason pulled in front of the nightclub where Sean's after party was being held. The line wrapped around the corner. Charlotte noticed the bouncer was only letting in a few people at a time.

"Your names?" the bouncer asked when they walked up.

Jason gave him their names and they were allowed entrance into the club. Current R & B and Hip-Hop music blasted over the loud speakers, as Jason led them to the VIP area.

"Jason, who's this pretty lady you have with you?" One of the bouncers who knew Jason said, while removing the black cord so they could enter the designated VIP area.

"This is my boss, Charlotte. Charlotte, this is Raphiel."

"Hi, Raphiel."

"How do you put up with this dude?" Raphiel asked.

"It's hard, but I manage." Charlotte laughed.

Raphiel looked down at his clipboard. "You two are on the list to sit at the big table set up for our guest of honor. I got word that he will be here in another hour. There's *hors d'oeuvres* and drinks."

"Thanks, man," Jason replied.

The tables were decorated with purple, black and white balloons. A bottle of expensive champagne sat on the top of each table.

Jason held Charlotte's seat as she sat down. "Would you like to snack on something? I'm famished."

"Sure. Put a little of everything on the saucer," Charlotte said.

"I'll be right back."

Charlotte pulled out her cell phone and saw she had several text messages. She responded to them while waiting on Jason's return.

"So we meet again," she heard a familiar voice say from behind her.

She looked up and it was Terrance Beckham, Mona's boss.

He took a seat next to her.

"How are you doing?" she asked.

"I'm fine. Just came from the concert. I tried to get your attention there, but there were so many people, you couldn't hear me over the noise."

"Yes, the women were going crazy."

"He has what they like. I understand you're his manager. Am I correct?" Terrance asked.

"Yes, you are."

"I want to offer your client a role in my next film. That is, if he can act."

"You have my card. Email me the script and I'll discuss it with him. When do you need to hear back from me?"

"I want to have my lead actors nailed down by the end of the month."

"Send me the script and shooting dates and I'll be in touch."

"Terrance, there you are." a woman wearing a too-tight dress and a little too much make-up said as she walked over and placed her hands on Terrance's shoulder.

She looked down at Charlotte and rolled her eyes. Charlotte snickered. She would bet her last dollar the next time she saw Terrance, she wouldn't be seeing him with this woman.

Terrance stood. "Charlotte, I look forward to hearing from you. Come on, Eva. There're a few more people I need to speak with."

Eva placed her arm around Terrance to let everyone know he was with her. Jason returned with her food. They discussed the concert while eating. "Sean left a lot of those women with their panties soaked."

"I'm trying to eat," Charlotte said.

"I'm just saying. Right now he's at his peak. I've come up with a name for his fragrance. We can call it 'Wet.'"

"I don't like it. Come up with something else," Charlotte suggested.

"If you have a better suggestion, let me hear it."

"In fact, I do. I was thinking about the name 'Magnetic'. It could be used for both the men and women's fragrances."

Jason rubbed his temple. "I like that. I'll run it by our study group and let you know what they think."

"Good. I think we have the name. Now we just need the right scent."

"So what did you think of Sean?"

"Sean's a client. Nothing more. Nothing less," Charlotte responded, in between bites.

"I was talking about his performance. But now you got me curious." Jason leaned on the table.

Before they could finish their conversation, the noise level intensified.

Charlotte turned around to see what all of the commotion was about. Sean and his band members, along with Priscilla walked inside of the VIP area. She watched as people gathered around him, wanting pictures and autographs.

Sean looked in her direction and smiled. She stood and walked towards him. "I enjoyed your show," she said.

"Did you like the song I wrote for you?" he asked.

"Which song was that?"

"All of them." He smiled and laughed.

"In that case, yes. I loved every single one of them." Charlotte laughed.

Being around Sean made her hormones go crazy. He was like a natural aphrodisiac. But aside from that, she loved how he made her feel. He trusted her, treated her like a princess and made her feel beautiful. The last thing Charlotte wanted to do was lose Sean. She really cared for him. She had to let him know how she felt before it was too late.

# Chapter Twenty-Seven

Sean spent the next few hours talking and taking pictures with peers and fans. He noticed Charlotte sitting at the table by herself.

"Right now, my mind is somewhere else," he said to Rocky, a popular rapper from his hometown of Houston.

Rocky looked in the same direction Sean was looking. "She's thick like we like 'em in Texas."

"That's my manager," Sean uttered.

"Then you don't mind if I walk over there and give her my number," Rocky said.

"As a matter of fact, I do mind."

"That's what I thought. So what's up with y'all?" Rocky asked, while women walked around them.

"The hell if I know."

Ironically, the song by Tamar Braxton, "Love and War" played throughout the club.

"Throw some of that southern charm on her. Go get your woman," Rocky commanded.

Sean took a big swig of his glass of Cognac and walked over to Charlotte.

"Dance with me," he said. Charlotte looked around the room. "It's a fast song. Nobody's paying us any attention."

Jason said, "Dance with the man."

"Fine. Come on." Charlotte stood and walked to the dance floor.

One of Rocky's songs played and everyone near him started yelling,

"Rocky...Rocky."

Sean liked the way Charlotte moved as she swayed her hips from side to side. He felt himself getting aroused when she backed up on him.

Charlotte turned around and faced him. "You can't handle all of this."

"We both know I can," Sean whispered in her ear as he held her close.

One of Sean's mid-tempo songs with a reggae beat played. The dance floor got jam-packed. Everyone, including Sean and Charlotte, did some of the dances from the video. When the song ended, Charlotte said, "That's it for me. These heels weren't meant for dancing." They'd been out for four songs.

One of Sean's slow songs played in the background. "I'll rub your feet if you'll dance with me on this song."

"I don't think it's a good idea."

Charlotte walked and sat down in her seat, Sean sitting next to her. "I've had enough of this place. Let's get out of here so I can give you that foot massage I promised."

"I have a limo out front. I'm good."

Sean looked around the room. He saw Jason and waved his hand to get his attention.

Jason walked near him. "What's up?" Jason asked.

"I'll make sure Charlotte gets home. You make sure your limo driver is taken care of." Sean removed a couple of hundred-dollar bills from his wallet and gave them to Jason.

"Sure, dude. Charlotte, enjoy yourself," Jason responded.

"Although I've been upset with you, I can't stay mad at you," Sean leaned down and whispered in her ear.

"But—"

Sean placed his finger up to her mouth. "Shh. Let me say my good-byes and we can head out."

"What is everyone going to think?" Charlotte asked.

"You're my manager. It's not odd for us to be seen leaving together. Now chill out."

Sean walked around the VIP area one last time. When he finished, Charlotte was waiting for him near the stairway.

He grabbed her hand and held on to it as partygoers snapped pictures of the two of them leaving the club. The limousine driver held the door open. Charlotte got in first and Sean got in behind her.

Some of the women in the line outside of the club screamed his name.

He rolled down his window and waved at his fans as the limo rode by.

Sean reached for the bottom of Charlotte's legs and placed them on his lap. He removed her heels, tossing them on the limousine floor.

"Has anyone ever told you that you have some beautiful feet?" Sean asked.

Charlotte leaned back in her seat and closed her eyes as he rubbed the bottoms of her feet. She looked to be enjoying the massage.

"That feels good," Charlotte said.

"You know what else will feel good?" Sean asked.

"What?" Charlotte asked as she licked her bottom lip.

"This." Sean pulled her into his arms and parted her lips with his tongue. Their tongues wrapped around each other as their breathing increased. Kissing Charlotte wasn't enough. He had to have her. He stopped kissing her long enough to look into her eyes. He could see that she wanted him as much he wanted her. When he slid her pants down revealing lace panties, he got no resistance. Instead, she helped him unbuckle his belt and without taking them completely off, he positioned himself over her. She gasped out in pleasure the moment he entered her.

"Oooh, Charlotteeee," he moaned, as he moved up and down inside of her.

Charlotte's walls had a tight grip on him and it didn't take long for him to spray his hot warm seed into her womb.

They held on to each other for a moment. Charlotte's head lay on his chest. He brushed the hair from her face. "Even when we don't see eye to eye, you've had my back. That really means a lot to me," Sean said.

Charlotte looked into his eyes. "I care about you, Sean. I want the best for you."

"Besides Marie, you're the only one who I feel truly does. I love you, Charlotte."

Charlotte touched his face. "I love you too, Sean."

Sean could see the love in her eyes. "I know you can't just drop everything and go out on tour with me, but I want you to meet me in Houston. We can make our relationship public then."

Charlotte shifted and got up off his chest. "Sean, I want to be with you, but now isn't the time."

"We just came from my after party. Nobody cared we were dancing together. Nobody will care if we are together. You are more concerned about appearances than you are about me."

"You know that's not true," Charlotte said, as she slipped back on her pants. She put the laced panties in her pocket. "You know I care."

"Then prove it. Meet me in Houston. I can introduce you as my woman on stage."

"No, that's not going to work," Charlotte retorted.

"So now we're back to square one," Sean said. He leaned back in his seat.

They rode the rest of the way to Charlotte's house in silence. The limousine pulled in front of her house.

"Talk to me. Say something," Charlotte requested.

"I don't know what else to say," Sean responded, without looking at her.

"Well then I guess…thanks for the ride," Charlotte kissed him on the cheek and then exited the limousine.

Charlotte tossed and turned the entire night. Guilt seeped into her conscience. They were having so much fun and she spoiled it by not giving in to Sean's request. A part of her hoped, he would have followed her inside but he didn't. Instead, she heard the limousine drive away with Sean in it. Charlotte was crushed. She had never felt this way about another man. Charlotte valued her privacy and saw firsthand what could happen when things went public. What if it didn't work out between them and he tried to ruin her? If only she could get

Sean to understand. What was so wrong with wanting keep her privacy? She saw how the intrusion of the media could ruin relationships. She didn't want that to happen to them. After holding her cell phone and going back and forth over whether or not she should call Sean, she finally hit the send button. The first time the phone rang out until she got voice mail. She ended the call and decided to call right back. This time her call was sent straight to voice mail. Not sure of what she wanted to say, she disconnected the call without leaving a message.

Her phone beeped indicating she had a text message. Sean's name displayed on the screen. She smiled...that is, until she read his words out loud. "I need to concentrate on my tour. If it's business, have Jason refer the message to me."

Her attempt to apologize backfired. She was disappointed he wouldn't talk to her. She needed to figure out a way to make things right with Sean. She cared about him and wanted to talk to him to see if they could reach some common ground. She hoped she wasn't too late.

Upset about how she may have messed things up with Sean, Charlotte put on some gloves and went to cleaning her house. She cleaned the windows, dusted, swept and mopped the floors. By the end of the day, she was exhausted.

She later took a long hot bath. Every time she closed her eyes, she fantasized about Sean sharing the bath with her. She'd recalled the last time he'd been in her bathroom and how gentle and soft his hands felt against her skin.

Charlotte leaned her head back and began to pleasure herself. She moaned Sean's name as she came to a climax.

The coldness of the water finally broke the trance. She got out of the tub, dried off and put on a pair of shorts and a t-shirt.

She needed to get her mind off Sean but he'd infiltrated himself into her world. There was only one thing that got her mind off her problems. She grabbed her laptop from the living room and her iPad. She logged online and checked her work emails.

She also needed to prepare for her meeting with Carmen. She'd asked Felicia to compile a list of all of Carmen's current clients. She opened the email with that information. She'd seen several familiar names such as Rose Purdue, the academy award-winning actress. She'd also seen Hailey Barnes' name on it. Although Hailey wasn't one of her favorite people, she would be a good client to have on her roster. The ex-model, now talk show host held the number one spot in ratings and from what she'd heard through the grapevine, was looking to explore other avenues in the world of entertainment.

Charlotte wanted to be a part of that. With the vision she had in mind, if Hailey listened to her, she could enhance her brand and there would be residual income for years to come for both of them.

Charlotte continued to go through Carmen's list of clients. In the ideal world, Charlotte would love to have all of Carmen's clients' transition to her firm, but she knew it wasn't realistic. Charlotte's strategy however was to at least obtain 90 percent of her big money makers along with some of her clients that were lesser known or considered on the D list when it comes to celebrity status.

Despite the excitement she felt about adding Carmen's clients to her roster, she couldn't help but think about how lonely it would be without Sean in her life. She picked up the phone to call him again, but didn't. She pushed her personal needs aside and thought it was best she waited because he didn't need any distractions. He needed to concentrate on his tour.

# Chapter Twenty-Eight

Sean poured himself into his work. His ego was far from being fragile, but there was just so much one man could take. There were women all over the world who would do anything for him. Who would help fulfill any one of his fantasies, but the woman he wanted, was unwilling to compromise and give him the type of commitment he desired.

It'd been almost a week since he'd seen Charlotte and sent her that text. His act of punishing her was also punishing himself. He wanted to talk to her, but thought he would give her a dose of her own medicine by not having any contact.

Bobby came inside of the Chicago venue dressing room. "It's almost show time."

"Give me a minute," Sean responded.

He stood and looked at his reflection in the mirror. The tight, black t-shirt accented his muscles. He had to get himself together. His fans counted on him to give a good show and that's what he would give them. He smiled and left the dressing room. The crowd yelled the moment he graced the stage. He gave a stellar performance at another sold out arena.

Sean ended the concert and exited the stage while the crowd cheered. He stopped and gave autographs and took pictures while making his way to his dressing room. Once behind the door, he closed his eyes and sighed in relief.

"Life's been treating you well," a blast from his past said, in a soft sweet voice.

Sean's eyes popped open. "Pandora, what are you doing here?"

Pandora, wearing a skin-tight, black, mini-dress, embraced him. "I couldn't let you come to my city without seeing you." Pandora gave him a quick peck on the lips.

A knock was heard at the door. Sean moved away from Pandora and opened it.

Priscilla walked in. "There's a reporter from the *Times* who wants to interview you. What do you want me to tell him?"

"Give me a few minutes and then bring him on in."

Priscilla looked Pandora up and down. "What are you doing here?" she asked.

Pandora looked at Sean. "Sean, I suggest you tell Ms. Cilla to mind her own business."

Sean ignored Pandora and said to Priscilla, "Can you get the reporter now, please?"

"Sure. What about her? You want me to get rid of her for you?" Priscilla asked.

Pandora moved from side to side. Sean stepped between the two women.

"No, I got this. You just take care of what I asked you to."

As soon as Priscilla was out the door, Pandora was in his face. "I can't believe you let her talk to me like that."

"Priscilla is harmless."

"She doesn't like me and I don't like her."

"She doesn't like you because you tried to use me, so chill out." Sean turned his back to Pandora. He couldn't ignore the fact that seeing Pandora again, brought back some old memories. Memories he didn't wish to revisit.

Sean picked up a clean towel off the table and wiped the sweat off his body. He went to the clothes rack and removed a black buttoned-down shirt from the hanger.

"You forgave me, so she should too." Pandora walked behind him and wrapped her arms around his waist.

He removed her arms and continued to button his shirt. "Look. I got this interview to do. If you want to hang out later, wait around. I'm supposed to be going to this after party at some club. If not, it's good seeing you again."

"I'll be waiting," Pandora said. She turned and shifted her hips from side to side as she walked to the door.

An hour later, Sean's limo pulled in front of one of Chicago's premiere clubs. The crowd was hyped when they noticed Sean and Pandora getting out of the back of the limousine. Cameras flashed.

"We love you, Sean," a lady nearby screamed.

Sean stopped and gave her a hug. "I love you too."

"Can I get a picture with you?" someone else asked.

Sean took out his phone. "Why don't we see how many people we can get in this one picture?"

The crowd came together as Sean snapped the photo.

"I'm tweeting this now," Sean said, right before leaving his satisfied fans.

The party at the club was in full swing. Pandora did her best to occupy most of Sean's time throughout the night. Despite their past, he didn't protest. He enjoyed her company.

After leaving the club, they sat together in the back of his limousine. Sean turned to Pandora. "Where should I have the driver drop you off?"

Pandora rubbed his leg. "I was thinking about spending a little more time with you, if that's okay."

Sean opened the dividing window and said to the driver, "Take us back to the Omni."

"Sure thing," the limousine driver responded.

Pandora continued to rub his leg. She leaned in to kiss him but Sean turned his head. "Hold up."

Pandora shifted her dress upwards, exposing the fact she wasn't wearing underwear. "Don't act like you don't want it."

Sean pulled her dress down. "There's no denying you're still sexy, but my heart's committed to someone else."

"She doesn't have to know. I'll be discreet," Pandora assured him.

"If you want to hang out and talk, we can but I'm telling you now, sex is not part of the equation."

"Fine. But you can't blame me for trying. We used to be so hot together."

Sean agreed. "Yes, but that was then and this is now."

Pandora leaned back in her seat, pulled out her cell phone and started pressing her screen. Sean looked out his window with his mind on Charlotte. Despite her breaking his heart, he was still loyal to her and had hopes she'd come around.

# Chapter Twenty-Nine

Charlotte sat across from the fifty-year-old Carmen Cain. Carmen was the manager to people in all forms of entertainment. She was immaculately dressed in a black Liz Claiborne suit, freshly manicured nails and salon-fresh hair.

"Charlotte, thanks for meeting me here. This is one of my favorite spots. I like to come and people watch," Carmen said.

Charlotte looked around, impressed by the restaurant's decor. "I was happy to get your call. I wasn't sure how our last meeting went."

Carmen laughed. "I know I wasn't too talkative. I learned a long time ago that if you're talking, you can't listen. I needed to see what your overall career goals were for yourself as well as your clients before saying what I have to say."

"I hope I was able to address all of your concerns."

"I've been watching you for awhile. You're not afraid to stand up for your clients. In this business, you have to be strong, especially as a woman."

"Tell me about it," Charlotte said, as she sipped her iced-tea.

"Over the next few weeks, I'll be talking to all of my clients. I want to recommend you to them. I can't guarantee they will sign, but they trust my judgment so I'm pretty sure most will."

Charlotte smiled. "I want to make the process as smooth as possible. Whatever agreement you have in place will just transfer over to me. I can have my attorney get with your attorney to make sure all of the legal paper work is handled correctly."

"I do have one concern," Carmen admitted.

Charlotte hoped she wouldn't bring up Darryl.

"You currently have seven associates, am I correct?" Carmen asked.

"Yes, but I'm already in the process of hiring more."

"I think we can help each other in that area too." Carmen removed a folder from her tote, handing it to Charlotte. "Here's a list of people who are currently working for me but will be needing jobs once I close my office. I'm not recommending anyone who isn't a go-getter. I'm not one to tell you how many more associates you will need to handle your roster. Only you can do that."

Charlotte placed the folder near her purse. "You're a legend in my field so if you're recommending them, then I will definitely consider hiring some of them."

Carmen's phone beeped. "Hold on for a minute. I need to take this call."

Charlotte estimated from their conversation, she would need to hire at least seven more associates. While Carmen handled her business, Charlotte sent a quick text to Felicia calling an emergency staff meeting.

"Sorry about that. One of my clients, which may end up being yours, has gotten herself into some trouble. I'm not sure if you're familiar with Pandora, but she's an up and coming actress. She started off in videos but I've been able to place her in a couple of movies since then. She's up for a role in a drama series, but this drunk driving charge might hurt her chances."

"Artists have to be careful these days with social media. Companies are more conscious about taking on clients with negative press."

"Indeed they are, that's why we have to stay one step ahead of the drama. I hate to cut our meeting short, but this is something I need to handle." Carmen placed a hundred dollar bill on the table. "This should take care of lunch."

"Thank you. But you've already done so much. I can pay the tab," Charlotte offered.

"No, dear. This one's on me," Carmen said, right before walking away.

Charlotte returned to the office feeling jovial.

Felicia met her at the door. "I'm so glad you're here. Jason's been looking for you."

"Did you schedule the meeting?" Charlotte asked.

"Everything's all set."

"I need you to cancel the employment ads. I got a list of potential employees right here." Charlotte waved the folder with the list of names in front of Felicia. "I want you to get me information on each one of them. Please have it ready for me by the end of the day."

Felicia didn't look too happy. "This is a lot of names. I'm not sure I can finish this by the end of the day."

"There's a bonus for you if you do but if not, no later than noon tomorrow."

"Sounds good." Charlotte headed to Jason's office.

"Knock...knock. Felicia said you needed to see me."

"Yes. You might want to have a seat for this." Jason had a worried look on his face.

Charlotte took a seat next to Jason's desk. He turned the computer screen around so that Charlotte could get a clear view. There was a picture of Sean and the actress, Pandora, leaving a club in Chicago.

"Let me get over there," Charlotte said. She and Jason switched seats.

Charlotte read the blog aloud. "'Are Mr. Naughty and the former Video Vixen a couple? After leaving the club, sources say Pandora was seen outside of Sean's hotel the next morning. We'll keep you informed when we learn more.' She didn't look drunk here so I don't know why others are reporting she got pulled over for a DWI."

Charlotte felt her heart drop. If Sean cared so much about her and wanted a commitment with her then why was he hanging out with this woman?

"This is not the kind of press Sean needs right now," Jason said.

"Sean's not the one with the DWI charges, this Pandora woman is," Charlotte responded.

"I've spoken to Sean. He's in Detroit now. He was unaware Pandora had been pulled over for DWI. He said she was sober when she left."

"So the part about her being at the Omni was true." Charlotte asked the question out loud but wasn't really expecting a response.

"I'm afraid so," Jason admitted.

"Get Sean on the phone for me. He and I need to talk." She was upset but

125

not for the reason Jason thought she was. She was upset because her rejection of Sean could have led him into the arms of another woman. She needed to get to the bottom of things.

Jason stood, reached across Charlotte and picked up his phone. "Anything for you, boss lady."

"Sean, it's Jason. Charlotte needs to talk to you."

Jason handed Charlotte the phone and left.

# Chapter Thirty

Sean sat on the edge of the hotel bed and listened to Charlotte's concerns from the other end of the phone.

"You need to be careful about the people you hang around. Jason's issued a short statement on your behalf."

Sean bent down to tie his new pair of Jordan's. "Anything else?" Sean asked.

"Yes. What is she doing coming out of your hotel room at eight o'clock in the morning? You know people are watching you. I've seen pictures of you online."

"Are you jealous?" Sean asked. He smiled.

"I'm only asking because as your manager it's my job to make sure you don't tarnish your image."

"Let's see. I'm a sexy R & B singer with women of all ages and races lusting after me. It's not odd to see any woman coming from my hotel room. In fact, it's expected."

Charlotte stuttered, "Just make sure you're more discreet next time."

"If there's nothing else, I need to make a stop at the radio station before heading to the concert venue."

"No, that's all."

Sean could have easily put Charlotte's mind at ease by being clear that he didn't have sex with Pandora but instead, he disconnected the call without waiting on Charlotte's response.

Priscilla knocked on his hotel room door.

"Come in," he yelled.

"The limo's waiting for us," Priscilla said.

"I'm coming."

After the radio interview, Sean performed to another sold-out arena in Detroit. Fans flocked to him afterwards.

Over the next couple of months, Sean went from city to city giving his fans a show they would never forget. The celebrity bloggers posted pictures and gossip during each stop of his tour. He was seen partying with a different woman just about every night or so it appeared.

What the paparazzi didn't know was he spent most of his time working on new songs for his next album. He hung with his band members and fans after each concert. When the tour ended, and he returned to Los Angeles, Sean planned on having a heart to heart talk with Charlotte. This time, he would not let her go.

Sean looked out the window of the roaring jet as it prepared for landing. He could see the downtown Houston skyline from his window. He smiled. He'd come to the place where he grew up. The place he once called home.

Fans and reporters met him as soon as he got off the plane. While his road manager and crew got their luggage, Sean signed autographs, talked to reporters and took photographs with those around him.

"I'll see y'all tonight at the concert," Sean said, as he waved and followed Priscilla and Bobby to their waiting limousine.

"Being home and getting this kind of love from everyone has really touched me," Sean marveled.

"You worked hard to get here. This is your time. Enjoy it," Bobby said. "I know I sure am."

"Thanks, man. You've been my road dog since day one. Remember traveling to the little hole-in-the-wall clubs?"

"They paid money but nothing like what you're getting paid now," Bobby reminded.

Sean spent the next twenty-four hours visiting family and making public appearances. He's stopped at several of his neighborhood schools and talked to the kids. He popped into one of the popular hip-hop radio stations and was the guest deejay for an hour. Sean loved his hometown and enjoyed being Houston's pride and joy.

The day of the concert, he met with his band to do a sound check. It took a little longer than expected to get it right, but once they did, it helped ease some of his anxiety. He didn't want anything to go wrong, leaving nothing to chance.

Right before the concert, he met with a group of children from his neighborhood and took them shopping. News cameras followed them, but the kids were still able to enjoy themselves. Sean felt good knowing he could give back to his community in some way.

The Houston traffic caused him to be late getting to the concert venue. Bobby had the opening act add ten minutes to their set. Shaka, another local R & B talent, didn't complain. She sang two more songs and prepared the crowd for Sean's appearance.

Sean changed into a pair of black slacks and a black satin shirt. He kept on his white tank top underneath it.

He went through his ritual of saying a prayer before leaving the dressing room and headed into the hallway.

Bobby walked up to him and said, "I was just about to come get you. Show time."

One of the popular deejays from a local radio station announced, "Here's what you all came for. Houston's own. Sean Maxwell!"

The band started playing.

"Houston, it's been a long time but here I am. It's a dream come true for me to be headlining this tour. I want you to know I got nothing but love for my hometown. H-town, this song's for you."

Sean sang and worked the stage while the background dancers also wooed the crowd.

Sean performed for an hour and a half. By the end of his show, he was shirtless and the women went wild. Bobby ran out on stage and handed him a black t-shirt. He slipped it on over his head.

Sean said, "Thank you, Houston, for showing me love. Peace."

Another voice was heard and the Mayor of Houston walked out, "Sean Maxwell, on behalf of the city of Houston, I'm here to give you the key to the city. Today has been declared Sean Maxwell Day."

Sean shook the mayor's hand, accepting the plaque with his name and the date engraved on the front of it. Sean kissed his two fingers and threw it towards the crowd. "Thank you, H-town. I'm out."

The crowd roared. Sean walked backstage with the mayor and they posed for a few pictures.

He mingled with other fans and celebrities who lived in the area.

"Water, please," Sean said to Priscilla.

Priscilla left and returned with a cold bottle of water.

"Excuse me for a minute." Sean opened the bottle and drank the entire thing. He went back to posing for pictures.

He saw his older sister, Marie, walking towards him. He ran to her and picked her up off her feet with a tight hug.

She playfully hit him. "Boy, put me down."

"How did you like the show?" Sean asked.

"I would have liked it better if it had been that sexy Trey Songz on stage instead of you."

"You've always been a hater," Sean teased.

"You did well. I'm proud of you, little brother." Marie touched his biceps. "Well, you're not really little anymore."

Sean flexed his muscles.

"Boy, you need to stop showing out in front of these women."

"We got people waiting on you," Priscilla walked over to remind him.

"The club's not going anywhere. Chill out."

Priscilla stepped back. "Hey, Marie, I'm sorry. I was so focused on getting Sean where he needs to be, I didn't even recognize you."

"No problem." Marie hugged Priscilla.

"Ok, let me get out of here. Got some phone calls to make. Good seeing you," Priscilla said to Marie. She dialed a number on her phone and placed it to her ear as she walked away.

Sean stepped in the changing area to change clothes. "You want to hang with your little brother tonight?" Sean asked.

"I'll pass. Just be sure you stop by tomorrow before you leave," Marie said.

Sean returned in a pair of black jeans, white t-shirt and black leather jacket. He walked from behind the curtain and gave Marie a hug and kiss on the cheek. He followed her out and made sure she got into her limousine. He got in the limo parked behind it and headed straight to the after party being held in his honor.

# Chapter Thirty-One

Charlotte eased her way through the crowded Houston club. She looked around until she saw the VIP area. She ran into a few people she knew along the way. She spoke to them and took a few pictures.

"You must be looking for my boy," Rocky, the rapper said, as she made her way towards the VIP section of the club.

"Hey, Rocky."

They greeted each other with a hug.

"Sean's on the other side of the club. People keep hounding him for pics." He pointed to the right side of the club.

"Thanks. I'll find him."

Charlotte went in the direction Rocky pointed. Her eyes locked in on Sean. Several women surrounded him. Some were very close to Sean. One was practically in his lap. Charlotte watched him laugh. He didn't seem to mind the attention, in fact, he looked to be enjoying it. One woman whispered in Sean's ear and he tilted his head back and let out a hearty laugh.

Charlotte walked closer to get Sean's attention but before she could get near him, Pandora brushed past her. She walked up to Sean as if she had a right to be with him, grabbed his head and kissed him. Sean didn't appear to resist her. In fact, it looked as if he was enjoying the kiss. Charlotte stood nearby and watched the exchange. Tears welled in her eyes and spilled down her cheeks before she could control them. Sean looked up and his intense gaze landed on Charlotte. Charlotte, feeling hurt, that she'd come to Houston prepared to apologize and make things right with Sean, couldn't run through the club fast enough. She rushed outside and called for her driver.

"Charlotte!"

She heard Sean calling her name but jumped in the back of the limousine as soon as it pulled up.

"Please hurry!" Charlotte yelled as she closed and locked the door behind her. Tears rolled down her cheeks.

Sean made it to the passenger door while the driver was getting behind the wheel. Charlotte watched him pull on the handle.

"I said hurry," Charlotte yelled at the limousine driver.

He pulled away from the curb almost knocking Sean over, but she didn't care.

Charlotte cried the entire drive to her hotel and ignored Sean's phone calls as she searched online for flights back to Los Angeles.

The driver pulled in front of the hotel, parked and opened her door.

"Wait here."

Charlotte rushed and packed in a hurry, practically falling over herself in her mad dash from the hotel. The driver remained out front as requested. He helped her with her bags and drove her to the airport.

Charlotte checked in and made it to her gate just in time to board her flight. She didn't exhale until she was tucked safely under the covers of her own bed. Exhausted and hurt, Charlotte fell into a fitful sleep.

The sound of someone banging on her door woke her. Glancing at the clock, she realized she'd slept for ten hours.

She dragged herself out of bed and into her robe before answering the door. She peeked out of the curtain. Mona and Kem were standing outside.

"Open up. We know you're in there. Your neighbor told us," she heard Mona say.

Charlotte opened the door. "That's what I get for having such a nosy neighbor."

They greeted her with a hug. Kem burst out, "You look a mess."

Mona grabbed her arm. "But that's not why we're here. You've been working hard and deserve a day of pampering."

Kem looked down at the luggage near the front door. "Going somewhere?"

"Let me shower and put some clothes on and I'll tell you everything," Charlotte countered.

"We'll be here when you get out," Mona said. "And after you dress, we're going to the spa. We can talk while getting our massages."

An hour later, they lay side-by-side as Charlotte told them what happened.

"You can't be mad at Sean," Kem said, being the voice of reason.

"She's right. In fact, you overreacted," Mona surmised.

Charlotte turned in their direction. "Whose friends are you? You're supposed to be on my side."

Kem spoke out. "When you're right, I will back you. But, Char, dear, you handled that situation all wrong."

Mona said, "To me, it looked like a misunderstanding. You should have stayed around to see what was going on. You can't be mad at him for socializing."

"But you didn't see all those women on him and the kiss." The thought of seeing Sean kiss another woman made her cringe.

"You said yourself that Pandora walked over to him. It wasn't like he initiated it," Kem pointed out.

"He didn't push her away either," Charlotte noted.

"If he was so into Pandora, he wouldn't have left her to run after you," Kem theorized.

"He's tried to do things the right way, but you turned him down. So, Charlotte, deal with it," Mona said, matter of factly.

Charlotte let their words marinate. She closed her eyes, trying to tune them out. Maybe she did overreact. Maybe she should have stayed and talked to him. Instead of being here with her friends, she could be enjoying time with Sean.

"I love Sean. I have to figure out a way to make things work," Charlotte said.

"If there's something you need us to do, we've got you," Kem assured her.

"I'm going to figure this out," Charlotte insisted.

"Now that your problem is semi-solved, let me tell y'all about my egotistical boss. He's a womanizer. He's a workaholic and he gets on my nerves," Mona said.

"Then find you another job," came from Kem.

"If you hired me as a writer on your show, I could do that," Mona responded.

"Mona, we've had this conversation before. The last time I hired a friend, I got burned. I like to keep my personal life separate from business. You know I like your writing and will give you glowing recommendations but we can't work together."

"One day, you're going to regret those words," Mona said.

"Ladies, where's the love?" Charlotte asked.

Mona pointed at herself, then at Kem and back at herself. "Love don't live here anymore."

"Stop playing. I love you like a sister," Kem said.

"Like Cinderella's step sister," Mona added, and then laughed. She looked at Kem. "I'm just kidding with you. I understand your rules, I just don't like them."

Charlotte and Kem listened to Mona's long rant about the struggles of being a screenwriter.

Later on that night, Charlotte lay in bed thinking about her conversation with her besties. Maybe, they were right. Maybe the kiss was just one big misunderstanding. Maybe she was overreacting and needed to give Sean a chance to explain himself. Her hand flew up to her head as it pounded. She didn't know what to believe.

# Chapter Thirty-Two

Sean tried his best to enjoy the rest of the weekend with his sister, Marie. But he couldn't help but think about Charlotte. He had no idea she was in Houston. Priscilla informed him after the fact that Charlotte had been at the concert. She claimed she forgot to tell him Charlotte would be meeting him at the club later.

Pandora kissing him caught him off guard. He didn't even know Pandora was in Houston. By the time he'd realized what was happening, he'd seen Charlotte standing there. He thought she was a mirage. He tried going after her but couldn't catch her before she got into the limousine.

His calls to Charlotte had been rejected so he decided to stop calling and wait until he got back to Los Angeles to see her face to face.

Marie walked Sean to the door of the large three-bedroom home he'd bought her when he signed his first record deal.

"Do I need to come out there and talk to this Charlotte?" Marie asked.

"Sis, I got this."

"I don't like seeing you hurt."

Sean shrugged his shoulders. "I'll put this southern charm on her when I get back. She'll come around."

He hugged and kissed Marie on the cheek. "Love you," she said, holding him in a tight embrace.

"Love you too, baby girl."

Leaving Marie behind was hard. He wished he could talk her into moving to Los Angeles. He really needed his family around.

Ten hours later, Sean was back in his Los Angeles home. It was too late to go to Charlotte's, so he decided to reach out to her the next day.

Sean got up early the next morning fully refreshed and on a mission. He dressed in one of his custom-made, gray Italian suits. He slipped on a pair of black socks and tied his black, leather dress shoes.

He met Priscilla in the hallway. "Where are you going this morning?" Priscilla asked.

"Out. If something comes up, text me; otherwise, I'll be busy," Sean responded.

He grabbed the keys to his Maybach.

As he neared his destination, he made a quick call. "Thank you for making the appointment for me. I'm pulling into the parking lot now."

Sean parked his car and less than ten minutes later, he was walking into the waiting area of Charlotte's office.

Felicia greeted him with a smile. "She doesn't know it's you, but she's ready for you."

Sean responded, "Thanks for doing this for me."

"I knew there was something going on between y'all. I'll do anything for love. Go get your woman," Felicia said, as she stood smiling from ear to ear.

"I hope you don't get into any trouble on my account."

"Don't worry about me. I keep this office running like a well oiled machine. Charlotte's not going to get rid of me. In fact, later, she'll be thanking me."

Sean crossed his fingers. "Let's hope."

"Good luck," Felicia said, as Sean walked away.

Sean knocked on Charlotte's door.

"Come in," Charlotte responded.

Sean took a deep breath and entered Charlotte's office.

Charlotte's mouth dropped open when she laid eyes on him. "What are you doing here? You can't be here. I have a meeting in a few minutes."

"I know. I'm your eleven o'clock appointment." Sean walked in and closed the door.

"Wait until I get my hands on Felicia." Charlotte stood and walked from behind her desk.

"It's not her fault. I asked her to do it." Sean walked towards Charlotte bringing them within inches of each other.

"You're not supposed to be here," Charlotte said, as she bit her bottom lip.

Sean reached down and grabbed Charlotte's hand. "You came to Houston for a reason. Why?"

"Houston was a big mistake," Charlotte said, as she looked into his eyes.

"I wasn't expecting to see you there," Sean confessed.

"Obviously not. I guess you forgot you'd asked me to come." Charlotte jerked her hand away. She walked to the other side of her office and stood by the window with her back facing Sean.

"I don't forget anything I tell you. I didn't expect you to be there because you pushed me away. There's only so much a man can take."

Charlotte turned to face him. Sean wanted to wipe her tear-filled eyes, but refrained from doing so. Instead, he kept his hands at his sides.

"I tried reaching out to you after that night, but you wouldn't talk to me," Charlotte said.

"I didn't want to hear any more of your excuses," Sean replied.

Charlotte walked to her desk and took a seat. Sean sat across from her.

Charlotte would barely look at him. "So is that why you hooked up with Pandora?"

"There's nothing going on between me and Pandora."

"Obviously she thinks so otherwise she wouldn't be kissing you." Charlotte folded her arms.

"Pandora's still upset I turned down all of her advances. And you want to know why? Because I don't care about her. I care about you. I want to be with *you*."

Charlotte uncrossed her arms. "You sure about that?"

"She caught me off-guard. If you would have stuck around you would have seen me push her away."

"Maybe you did. I don't know. All I know is I saw her put her tongue down your throat."

"Read my lips. I do not want Pandora. That kiss you saw wasn't what it looked like. She kissed me. I didn't kiss her."

"Well, what about the photos of you with all those women?"

Sean threw his hands in the air. "Most of my fans are women. I know you're not tripping over something like that."

Charlotte grabbed her iPad, tapped the screen a few times, and then held it up. "Chicago, you were there with Miss luscious lips Pandora. Miami, you were seen cuddled up with some stripper. New York, you were with Monet, who you swore nothing was going on with. And of course, you and Ms. Pandora were seen again in Houston. I guess the celebrity bloggers didn't catch the kiss you two shared, but I sure did. Should I go on?"

Sean leaned his head back and laughed. "You are so jealous. Don't you know none of those women hold a candle to you? You are it for me. I don't know what else I have to say or do to prove it to you."

"I came to Houston because I wanted to make things right between us," Charlotte said.

"So are you saying you're willing to give me what I want?"

Charlotte looked away. "Maybe we should talk about this later."

"Your schedule's cleared for the next two hours. So I'm sitting here until you give me an answer." Sean leaned back in his chair, crossed his arms, and stared at Charlotte without blinking an eye.

Charlotte got out of her seat and went to the door.

"Don't leave," Sean begged.

"I'm not." Charlotte clicked the door, locking it.

She began unbuttoning her blouse as she walked back to where Sean sat. She stood before him as he looked at her with his mouth open. "I want you." She straddled him. "I missed you."

Charlotte planted kisses on Sean's face. Sean pulled away. "I want a full commitment from you. I want to be able to claim you as mine and me, yours. I'm tired of this merry go round. I want to merge our lives together and love you the way you deserved to be loved."

Charlotte rubbed his face. "I know now it's also what I want."

"There are going to be times I want to take you out."

"No problem. We just can't show any public display of affection. No need to draw attention to ourselves," Charlotte responded.

Sean picked up her hand and kissed the back of it. "I shouldn't agree to this, but I want you in my life so bad that I'm willing to compromise."

"Oh and another thing, you have to make it known to all your scandalous female admirers that you are no longer on the market."

"Anything for you, my dear. How do you want to celebrate?" Sean asked, right before kissing Charlotte on the neck. "Like this." His kisses trailed down her chest. "Like this." He freed one of her breasts from her bra, brought her stiff nipple to his lips, and sucked on it.

Charlotte leaned her head back and moaned. "Don't stop."

Sean lifted her out of the chair and placed her on the love seat located on the other side of the room in her office. He removed her clothes. "I just want to look at you," he said, as he watched her while taking off his expensive suit and discarding it on the floor.

Charlotte looked at Sean's stiff erection and got moist in between her legs.

He leaned over her and Charlotte used her hand and helped push him inside of her. She wrapped her legs around him and they made love. She closed her eyes and the mental orgasm turned into a physical one as her whole body shook with pleasure. They sealed the deal. Sean and Charlotte were now officially a couple.

# Chapter Thirty-Three

Charlotte rested her head on Sean's chest. He brushed her hair back so he could look into her eyes. "I love you, Charlotte." He kissed the top of her forehead.

"I love you too, Sean," Charlotte responded. "Thank you for not giving up on me...on us," She squeezed her arm around him.

"As much as you hurt me, I couldn't give up on you. I knew you loved me too. You've always had my back. Even when we weren't seeing eye to eye. I smile from the inside out knowing you truly care about me."

Sean and Charlotte kissed again. Charlotte eased up from on top of him. "Next time, we might not want to make love in the office, in the middle of the day when everyone's here."

She reached down and gathered her underwear, skirt and blouse from the floor.

"You seduced me." Sean sat up and smiled.

"We can wash up in the bathroom."

Sean looked at her and found himself getting aroused again. "You go first. I'll wait right here. If we go in the bathroom together, there will be a round two."

"You're right. I have a staff meeting this evening. I got the contract from Terrance. When we're both dressed, we can sit and discuss it."

Charlotte and Sean got re-dressed and sat across from each other as Charlotte went over the contract.

"You sure I should do this movie? I'm not an actor," Sean conceded.

"Terrance sees something in you. If you're feeling uncomfortable about it, why don't you let me register you for an acting class?"

"Will it be discreet? I don't want people knowing about it," Sean said.

"I am signing a new client. The actress, Rose Purdue. I can ask her to give you some pointers. Are you willing to work with her?" Charlotte asked.

Sean knew Rose was married to Lance King, a music producer he'd worked with on his second album. Working with music producers Lance and Casper garnered him hit after hit. Sean had nothing but gratitude for them both.

"Sure. Maybe then, I'll feel more comfortable about taking the role," he responded.

"Sean, you can do this."

Sean smiled, happy that Charlotte believed in him. "Let me see a pen."

Charlotte handed him a black ink pen before picking up her cell phone. "Okay, ready."

Charlotte snapped a picture of him signing the contract. She posted it to her social media pages with the caption: Sean Maxwell is about to take it to the next level.

Sean handed her the paper. She placed it back in a manila folder. "I'll get this sent over to Terrance and once we get his signature and a copy of the contract, it will be official."

"You better get Rose on the phone right away. I need to start practicing."

"Hold on."

Sean leaned back in his chair and watched Charlotte talk to Rose about mentoring him. He loved to watch her work. Charlotte ended the call. "We're all set. Rose says she can meet with you tomorrow."

"Great. Thanks, Charlotte."

"I'm just doing my job. Speaking of which, now that you're back, Jason wants to discuss a world tour. And he just got the fragrance samples in for you to check out."

"You guys have been busy. I'll stop by his office before I leave."

"He's meeting with Casper and Parris Mitchell right now at their residence. I'll have him call you."

"Sounds good."

"I think for the day to day management, Jason will continue to manage you. I'll step in when need be. Like in the case of this movie deal with Terrance's production company."

"That sounds like a reasonable compromise," Sean said.

"I would hate to lose you as a client."

Sean leaned forward. "Baby, you don't have to worry about me going anywhere. I'm yours in *every* way."

Charlotte shifted in her seat. "You're being naughty again."

"They don't call me Mr. Naughty for nothing." Sean licked his lips, got up and leaned across the desk. "Give me some sugar."

She exhaled as he kissed her lips. "I can get used to your kisses."

"Good. Because I plan to kiss you as many chances as I can get. But, sweetheart, I know you've got work to do and I've got a few things to take care of myself. Let me get out of here."

Sean walked out of Charlotte's office as Charlotte's man and with his first acting role. Sean wanted to do something special for Charlotte to celebrate. When he left her office, he drove straight to Rodeo Drive in Beverly Hills.

He entered into a dress shop specializing in evening gowns. The sales clerks were about to run over themselves to get to him. The brown-haired woman said, "Sean Maxwell, I can't believe it's you."

The redheaded sales clerk asked, "Do you mind taking a picture with us?"

Sean smiled. "Only if you two can help me pick out an outfit for my girlfriend."

"What size does she wear?" the brown-haired woman asked.

"Not sure. But together I think we can figure it out."

The sales clerks showed him different dresses. After deciding on a royal blue dress with sequins around the waist area, Sean chose a size he believed would fit Charlotte. "I also need shoes and accessories to go with it," Sean said.

"Already two steps ahead of you. How do you like these?" The redhead showed him a pair of black stilettos with diamonds around the heel.

"I like those."

The brunette opened the top of a big black velvet box. "This is a ten carat diamond sapphire necklace and earring set I think any woman would love."

Sean ran his hand across the sapphire necklace and matching dangling earrings. "I'll take them. Ring them up, ladies. I would like to have them delivered today around seven o'clock."

Sean paid for his items and wrote down Charlotte's address. Before leaving the store, he took a few pictures with the clerks.

"Thanks again, ladies," he said, as he turned to leave.

He heard one of them say, "His girlfriend is one lucky woman."

*No, I'm one lucky man*, Sean thought.

# Chapter Thirty-Four

Charlotte had barely made it in the door, when she heard the doorbell ring. She looked out the peephole and saw a deliveryman holding a garment bag and, what looked like, a huge gift bag.

"Who is it?" Charlotte asked, without opening the door.

"Ma'am, I'm Jules. I have a delivery from Raves of Beverly Hills."

She opened the door. "There must be a mistake. I haven't ordered anything."

Jules looked at the note taped to the bag. "It's from Sean Maxwell. I was told to deliver it to you at seven. If you weren't here, I was supposed to wait for you."

"Give them here. I'll take them." Charlotte took the items and carried them inside.

Her heart dropped when she saw what was in the garment and gift bags.

Her cell phone rang. Sean's name showed on the display. "I was just about to call you."

"Do you like them?"

"Of course. How did you know my sizes?"

"With the help of two competent sales clerks," Sean responded.

"I can't wait to wear the dress," she said.

"Put them on tonight. I want to take you out to dinner to celebrate us."

"I can cook something and you can come over."

"No, baby. You've worked a long day. Let me do this, please."

"But, Sean, you don't have to take me to expensive restaurants or buy me expensive dresses to impress me. I'm fine relaxing at home."

"Allow me to romance you the way I want to," Sean cooed.

"I need a little time to get ready. Why don't you pick me up around eight? That'll give me time to shower, dress and do something with my hair."

"Can't wait to see how you look in that dress?"

"Neither can I," Charlotte responded.

Charlotte went straight to the bathroom after ending the call with Sean. She took a shower and grabbed the dress. She looked at the price tag on the dress.

"No way," Charlotte said out loud. "He paid five thousand dollars for this dress."

That was the most any man had ever spent on her. Charlotte felt nervous. This dinner with Sean was a turning point in their relationship. She needed to calm her nerves. She glanced at the clock and decided to call her two besties.

She called Kem and Mona on the three-way. She placed the phone on speaker and talked to them while she got dressed.

Charlotte spoke with excitement. "I wanted you both to know I took your advice and Sean and I are officially a couple."

Kem and Mona screamed with joy from the other end of the phone. They both started talking at the same time. Charlotte couldn't understand either one of them.

Mona squealed, "I'm so happy for you."

"It's about time, you listened to me," Kem added.

"Ladies, I just wanted to call and tell you that. I'm getting ready for a date with my man."

Kem asked, "What are you on the phone with us for? Get off and get dressed. Wear something sexy."

"Call me when you get in. I want details on how this date goes," Mona said.

"Bye, ladies." Charlotte walked over and hit the end button on her phone.

Charlotte went and stood in front of the floor length mirror behind her closet door. She pulled her hair back in a bun with a few strands of hair hanging from the side. Satisfied with her look, she removed the dress from the hanger and slipped it on.

The dress was just right. It accented all of her curves. She hoped Sean liked how she looked in it. She slipped on the heels just as the door bell rang.

"Coming," she yelled. She grabbed her keys and a small black clutch bag.

Sean stood on the other side of the door, wearing a black designer suit and a tie that matched her dress.

He greeted her with a hug and a kiss. "Let me look at you."

Charlotte walked and twirled for him.

"You look absolutely stunning," he marveled. "Makes me want to rip your dress off you and make love to you right here and now."

Charlotte shook her finger back and forth. "Oh no, mister. You wanted to go out, so you're taking me out."

"My queen will always get what she wants. Your chariot awaits you," Sean said, as he extended his hand.

Charlotte placed her hand in his and he escorted her out.

# Chapter Thirty-Five

Sean and Charlotte enjoyed laughter and mindless conversation over dinner at the ritzy yet secluded Italian restaurant located in the heart of the city. Reservations were usually made weeks in advance, but Sean pulled a few strings and got a reservation in less than an hour.

Charlotte took the last bite of her food and placed her fork down. She wiped her mouth with her napkin. "The food here is excellent," she remarked.

"I'm glad you approve," Sean said, as he motioned for the waiter.

"Yes, sir. Is everything to your satisfaction?" the blond-haired male waiter asked.

"Everything's great. Please bring us two strawberry crepes."

"Perfect choice," the waiter responded. "Let me get these out of the way, if you're finished."

Sean indicated with the nod of his head that they were.

The waiter removed their dinner plates and left them alone.

Sean looked at Charlotte. "I know how much you like strawberries, so you're going to love dessert. It's one of their signature dishes."

"So you think you know me," Charlotte teased, after taking a sip of her wine.

Sean looked across the table at her. "As much as you've allowed me to. I'm still waiting on you to take down those walls you have around your heart."

"I'm here with you now. Isn't that enough?" Charlotte asked.

"I want all of you," Sean responded.

Before Charlotte could respond, another waiter approached holding two saucers of strawberry crepes. He placed one in front of each of them.

Charlotte took a bite out of hers. She closed her eyes.

"So what do you think?" Sean asked.

"Scrumptious. I love it." Charlotte went back to eating her dessert.

"I'm glad you approve."

Thirty minutes later, they were inside of Sean's Maybach headed down the highway.

Sean glanced over at Charlotte periodically as he drove. It felt good to see her happy. He touched her hand and their fingers interlocked.

"This isn't the way to my house," Charlotte commented.

"I know," Sean responded. "The night's still young."

"Where are we going?" He noticed Charlotte looking at him from the corner of his eye.

"You'll see when we get there."

"Sean, I don't like surprises."

"You might as well get used to them, because I plan on surprising you a lot. This is only the beginning."

Sean pulled in front of Club Venus. Valet attendants rushed to open their doors.

Sean handed the valet closest to him a twenty-dollar bill. "Be extra careful with my baby."

"I'll take care of it as if it belonged to me," the man said as he smiled and got into the running car.

Sean walked to the other side of the car and reached for Charlotte's hand.

They walked up the walkway side by side. Sean paid for their entry into the club. The music was a mixture of Pop and R & B from the eighties and nineties. The crowd appeared to be a mixture of young and middle-aged people.

There were no vacant tables so they stood near the bar.

"Where did you find this place?" Charlotte asked Sean over the loud music.

"One of my band members told me about it. I like to come here when I don't want to be bombarded with fans. Most of the people here are in their own little world. They don't bother me and I don't bother them."

"I feel like I've stepped back in time," Charlotte said, as one of Gloria Estefan's songs came on. She swayed from side to side.

"Come on, let's dance. I can see you want to." Sean grabbed Charlotte by the hand and pulled her out onto the crowded dance floor.

They danced for thirty minutes straight. When the deejay slowed it down by playing a slow jam by Prince, Charlotte turned to walk away, but Sean reached for her hand and pulled her back towards him.

She looked at him. He wrapped his arm around her waist. She placed both of her arms around his neck. Sean found himself entranced with her. The lyrics to the song expressed the desire he felt.

People surrounded them on the dance floor but as far as he was concerned, no one else existed, but them.

Her thick pouted lips were too inviting not to taste. It took everything within him to resist. Charlotte laid her head on his chest. He pulled her closer to him. He inhaled the fresh citrus smell of her hair. He wanted to rub his hand through her hair. His restraints were weakening.

He whispered in her ear. "I've been trying to be good, but I don't know how much longer I can last."

Charlotte looked up at him and smiled. She laid her head back on his chest. They danced the next few songs.

The tempo got faster. "Let's sit this one out," Charlotte suggested.

This time he didn't stop her when she walked off the dance floor. He followed behind her.

"Let me find us a table," Sean said.

"I'm ready to go," Charlotte declared.

"I thought you were having a good time."

"I am, but I'm ready to spend some alone time with you," Charlotte responded.

Sean knew what she meant and he was not going to deny her that pleasure. "Come on, let's go."

Sean held Charlotte's hand and led her outside. He reached into his pocket and handed the valet his ticket.

They continued to hold hands and stare into each other's eyes and smile.

The valet drove his car and parked it in front of them. As promised, Sean gave the man a nice tip.

"Your place or mine?" Sean asked, once they were pulling out of the parking lot.

"Surprise me." Charlotte winked.

# Chapter Thirty-Six

A few days later, Sean sat behind his computer surfing the internet. He gleamed with pride as he read the reviews from his tour. He couldn't wait to finalize the details on his world tour. He wanted the opportunity to meet his fans overseas. He wished he could convince Charlotte to go with him, but he knew she wouldn't be able to leave her business for that long period of time.

It was Friday and he was preparing for his second meeting with Rose Purdue. He never imagined he would be taking acting lessons from Lance's wife.

Lance and Sean were around the same height. They gave each other a firm handshake as Lance invited Sean into their home.

"Rose is busy with the twins right now, but she'll be down in a minute. So you've gotten the acting bug, huh?" Lance said, as he led Sean into what appeared to be a den.

"Yes, my agent thinks it's a good idea. It couldn't hurt. In fact, it'll only increase my fan base."

"Well, if anyone can teach you, it's my wife. She's the best," Lance gloated.

"That's why I'm here," Sean said.

"Can I offer you anything?" Lance asked.

Sean shook his head. "No, I'm fine."

Rose walked in making a grand entrance. "Here's my star pupil."

Lance laughed. "He's your only student."

"And he's a star," Rose looked at him and smiled.

Sean stood and greeted Rose with a hug.

"The twins are sleeping, but I don't think they'll be down long."

"You take care of my boy here and I'll go make sure those boys of mine stay out of your way," Lance responded.

"He spoils those boys," Rose said.

"How old are they now?" Sean asked.

"Four going on forty-four." Rose laughed. "But enough about them. Let's talk about you. I want to see if you've been practicing since our last meeting."

"I'm a little nervous, but here it goes," Sean said. He stood and re-enacted a script she'd given him.

At the end of the scene, Sean watched Rose's expression. Her face was blank.

She sat down on the couch and patted the seat next to her.

Sean didn't like how things were going. "Give it to me straight. How bad was I?" he asked, as he took a seat.

"Not bad at all," Rose remarked. "I want you to listen to me. I'm going to be Zen and you read the mother's part."

After Rose and Sean reversed the roles, Rose asked, "Now do you see the difference?"

Sean nodded. "You got really into it."

"I want you to get to the point where you're one with the character. When I see you, I should see Zen, not Sean. Now let's try this again."

He got up and they reenacted the scene again. At the end, Rose clapped her hands.

"Sean, you nailed it." Rose walked to the desk and picked up a black binder. She glanced it and then handed it to Sean. "I want you to learn the rest of Zen's lines. Today's Friday, so I'll see you here on Monday. Same time."

The script was at least twenty pages long. "I need to know all of this by Monday?"

"Keep in mind that most scripts are ninety to hundred and twenty pages. So if you can't handle twenty pages, you might want to reconsider," Rose said.

"Never mind. I got this. It's just so new to me," Sean admitted.

"From what I can tell, you're a natural. Don't let anyone tell you differently.

All you need to do is continue to practice and remember what I said."

"Become one with the character," Sean recalled.

"You got it. If you can do that, forget the critics. You're going to nail the role and they will be singing your praises later," Rose said.

"You and Charlotte have so much confidence in me."

"We have to support our men."

Sean left Rose's feeling more confident about his acting abilities. He called Charlotte from the car.

"What are you doing tonight?" Sean asked.

"One of my clients is having a party, so I have to attend," Charlotte responded.

"It's not Parris' party, is it?"

"As a matter of fact, it is."

"Cool. I got an invite too. Now I know for a fact I'm going. What time do you want me to pick you up?" Sean asked.

"I have a conference call with another client so I'll just meet you there."

"I'll see you soon," Sean said, as he pressed the button on the steering wheel to disconnect the call.

# Chapter Thirty-Seven

Charlotte wished she had told Sean to come get her because after a long day at the office she didn't feel like driving. Plus, she couldn't wait to see him. It was too late to call a car service and too late to cancel, so she had no choice. She slipped on her slippers and pulled up her black dress with the split in it and slid behind the wheel of her car. She threw her stilettos and small clutch bag on the passenger seat.

Her plans to get to the party early changed when she got stuck in busy Los Angeles traffic. After an hour, she finally reached her destination. She drove to the front of Parris' house and gave her key to the valet. The valet attendant handed her a ticket. She replaced her slippers with her heels and walked inside.

She greeted people she knew with hugs, air kisses and handshakes. She saw the guest of honor busy in a corner surrounded by people. Parris held up her hand to get Charlotte's attention. Those gathered around Parris stepped aside as Charlotte entered the area.

Parris greeted her with a hug and kiss on the cheek. "So glad you made it. Everyone, this is Charlotte Richards. She's my new manager."

Everyone around them greeted Charlotte. She shook hands with each of them except, Carmen, with whom she shared a hug. "You can call this my farewell party. I'm passing on the torch to you now."

"I'm forever grateful." Charlotte placed her hand over her heart.

"There's Hailey Barnes. I need to introduce you two," Carmen stated. "Hailey, my dear. This is Charlotte. The woman who will be taking my place."

Hailey hugged Carmen and looked at Charlotte. "You can never be replaced," Hailey responded.

Charlotte extended her hand out to Hailey. "Our schedules have been conflicting. Maybe we can set something up for next week."

"Now that I've met you, let's make this happen. I have to admit I was a little skeptical at first," Hailey admitted.

"I understand. My goal is to make this an easy transition."

Carmen stepped between them. "No more shop talk. Hailey will be in touch with your office next week to schedule an appointment. This is a party, so let's party."

Charlotte noticed Hailey's gaze. "No wonder I felt my temperature rise a little. He's hot," Hailey uttered.

"I don't think Garrett will like the fact you're fiending over another man," Carmen said.

"Garrett and I have made love to Sean Maxwell's songs a million times. Garrett will probably give him a high-five."

"Where is your husband?" Carmen asked.

"Some foreign dignitary was having a party and he was short on people," Hailey responded.

"Hailey's husband owns a security firm. You've probably heard of it, GT Securities."

"I'm very familiar with his company. Some of my clients use their services.," Charlotte responded.

"Look. Mr. Naughty is coming our way," Hailey said.

Carmen removed herself from in between them. "I'm going to leave you two. I see someone I haven't seen in years. Take care, my dears."

Hailey walked closer to Charlotte. "Looks like he has his eyes on someone and to my surprise, it isn't me."

Charlotte ignored Hailey. Sean got closer. "Hello, ladies," Sean said.

Charlotte hoped Hailey couldn't hear her rapid heartbeat. Sean wore black so well. The all black suit seemed to accentuate his muscular frame. Charlotte's mind recalled how he looked without the shirt and blazer.

Hailey spoke first, "Mr. Maxwell. When are you going to come on my show? I heard you were up for a movie part, is it true?"

Sean plastered on a smile. "Hailey, I'm going to give you an exclusive right now. Charlotte, is it okay if I tell her?"

Charlotte responded, "Sure. Everything's official. The press release will be going out in about a week."

Hailey placed her hand up to her forehead acting as if she was going to faint. "OMG, I got an exclusive. Wait until my talk show audience hears this on Monday."

Hailey looped her arm through Sean's He had a "come rescue me" look on his face.

Charlotte laughed and shook her head, indicating no.

"I'm going to leave you two alone while Sean tells you his good news." Charlotte giggled to herself as she walked away.

Charlotte mingled with some of her peers and other celebrities in attendance. The live music, food and company were good. Charlotte went outside on the patio. With the location of the house, she was able to see the Los Angeles skyline.

"You will pay for leaving me alone, later on tonight," Sean walked beside her and said.

"Hailey is a piece of work," Charlotte said.

"If she could go on the air live tonight to tell her audience that it's confirmed I'm in Terrance's next movie, she would. You should have seen her salivating at the mouth."

"She's probably feeling that way because she beat out Wendy Williams by getting this exclusive," Charlotte concluded.

"Enough about Hailey, talk shows and all things concerning work. Let's talk about you and that killer dress. When I saw you standing there with your legs peeking out from under the split, I wanted to rush over and scoop you away in my arms."

"That would have given Hailey something other than your budding movie career to talk about." Charlotte laughed.

"Come with me," Sean said.

Charlotte looked back. No one appeared to be paying attention to them. Everyone was inside. Charlotte walked away with Sean further out on the patio but not in clear view of the house.

Sean pulled her into his arms and kissed her. When he came up for air, he said, "Now that I got that out of my system, we can go back inside."

Charlotte had to catch her breath. Sean's kisses always left her breathless.

Sean grabbed her hand and they walked back towards the patio doors.

When they got inside, Charlotte noticed lipstick smudged on Sean's lips. She grabbed a napkin off a nearby tray and handed it to Sean. "Wipe your mouth. Quick."

Sean did as instructed. Charlotte sighed with relief. She hoped no one else noticed them missing and returning back inside together. Her desire to keep their relationship private had become an obsession.

# Chapter Thirty-Eight

Sean and Charlotte went their separate ways. Each mingled with the guests. He'd only had one glass of champagne and the rest of the time he drank sparkling cider. He walked near Charlotte who'd been talking a little louder than normal. "Excuse us for a minute," he said, as he eased Charlotte away from the small crowd of people.

"What's wrong?" Charlotte asked.

"I noticed you getting a little loud. That's unlike you."

"I'm enjoying the party," Charlotte said, looking around.

Sean could smell the alcohol on her breath. "I think you've drunk too much. Come on. Let's get you out of here." Sean touched Charlotte's arm.

She jerked her arm away. "I will let you know when I'm ready."

"I'm only looking out for you. Like you look out for me," Sean said.

"Fine. Can you have them bring my car around?" Charlotte reached into her clutch and removed her ticket. It fell to the floor.

Sean picked it up. "I'll get your car. Meet me out front."

He handed the valet Charlotte's ticket. He said to one of the valet attendants. "I will send someone to get my car later."

"Yes, Mr. Maxwell," the attendant responded.

Charlotte walked outside as the valet returned her car. "This was a great party. I've made so many new contacts. Looks like you made a lot of contacts too." Charlotte slurred when she talked.

Sean knew then, he would definitely be driving and not Charlotte.

Sean walked over to the driver's side when the valet pulled up.

"I'm driving you home," Sean insisted.

"No. I can drive myself."

Sean turned and faced Charlotte, the smell of alcohol strong around her. "You're causing a scene and I know the last thing you want to do is draw attention to us."

She threw her arm in the air. "You win. Come on, let's go."

Charlotte walked to the passenger side and got in. Once inside, Sean leaned over Charlotte and placed on her seatbelt. He then secured his own belt and drove Charlotte home.

Charlotte talked non-stop about the party until they reached her place. He made sure she got inside. He helped her undress and placed her in bed under the covers.

Charlotte put her arms around his neck and pulled him down. "I want you, Sean. I've wanted you from the moment I saw you in the *Call Me Mr. Naughty* video. You exude sex appeal. I didn't start liking chocolate until I saw you do that dance...you know that thing you do with your hips."

Charlotte moved in the bed as if she was mimicking his signature dance. Sean tried to not laugh, but he couldn't wait until she was sober to remind her of this moment.

"What's so funny? I didn't find it funny seeing you with all those women tonight. I saw how they were lusting after you. I started to get on the intercom and tell them all they couldn't have you, because you are mine. You are mine, *aren't* you?" Charlotte asked.

"Yes, baby. I'm all yours," Sean responded.

He tried to ease away, but Charlotte wasn't having it. "Then show me. Make those other women jealous you're here with me."

This time Sean was able to free himself. "Charlotte, baby. There's no one here but you and I."

"Good. I like it better when we're by ourselves. I don't have to share you with the world."

Sean wanted to make love to Charlotte but not like this. He eased the covers over her shoulders and tucked her in.

He stood. Charlotte's eyes popped open. "Don't leave me."

"I'm going to make sure the doors are locked. I'll be right back. I promise," Sean said.

He did as he stated then went to the bathroom and washed up. He removed his clothes and when he re-entered the bedroom, he was wearing nothing but his boxers.

Charlotte was already asleep. Sean slid under the covers beside her and wrapped his arms around her. He soon fell asleep.

"Sean Maxwell, what happened last night and I demand to know now," were the first words Sean heard after awakening the next morning.

"Charlotte, calm down," Sean said. "You got a little drunk. I drove you home and that was it."

"You mean, you didn't make hot passionate love to me? No wonder I woke up feeling disappointed," Charlotte taunted. Then she laughed. "I don't know what came over me. I normally don't drink like that."

"I'm glad you weren't a sloppy drunk though because it wouldn't have been a good look for you. Good thing you had me there to come to your rescue before you got out of control."

"Thank you, Sean, for saving me."

Sean eased from under the covers and batted his puppy dog eyes. "Can I get a reward?"

"I'll think about it." Charlotte grabbed a pillow off the bed, hit Sean with it and ran out of the bedroom.

# Chapter Thirty-Nine

The hot stream of water in the shower felt good as Charlotte leaned back and closed her eyes.

She opened them when she felt Sean's hands roaming her soapy body.

"You didn't think you were going to get away that easily, did you?" he asked, as his hands touched her in sensitive spots.

Her back remained towards him as he played with her clit with one hand, kissing the nape of her neck at the same time. He brought her to the edge of an orgasm and then stopped. He turned her around and then bent down on his knees. He positioned her where he could devour all of her in his mouth. She almost lost her grip as her legs shivered and she came in his mouth with an intensity leaving her legs weak.

Sean held her as she gained her balance. They took turns washing each other off before exiting the shower.

Sean took the time to dry Charlotte off first and then dried himself. He wrapped the towel around his waist.

Charlotte licked her lips. She loved looking at him and knowing that one of the sexiest men she'd ever known wanted to be with her. He'd awakened something in her. When they were together, nothing else mattered. It was like they were in their own little world. She felt safe around him. For the first time, she'd found someone who had her back.

The more they made love, the more she wanted him. It's like she could never get enough of his love. She'd never felt that way about any man. This magnetic pull Sean had over her was undeniable.

Sean sat on the bed and watched her get dressed. "Charlotte, when I'm here with you, I feel like I'm at home."

"They say home is where the heart is," Charlotte said, as she pulled up her jeans and fastened them.

"You have all of me." Sean placed both of his hands over his heart.

Charlotte walked over and stood in between his legs. "I love you too, Sean Maxwell."

"She loves me." Sean fell back on the bed and pulled her down on top of him so that they were face to face.

Charlotte planted kisses on each side of his lips. "Yes, I do." She then kissed him on the lips.

She attempted to get up, but he wouldn't let her. "Come on, Sean. I need to get up. I want to cook you a nice breakfast."

"You're a full course meal," Sean said, as he kissed her on the neck.

She leaned back. "Baby, come on. I want to do this."

Sean stopped. "Okay. I'll stop. For now."

Charlotte stood. Sean sat up.

Charlotte asked, "What are you going to do about clothes?"

"I've got someone dropping off some clothes and my car."

"I'm not complaining. I love looking at you in nothing but a towel."

"There's somewhere I want to take you and I'm pretty sure clothes are required," Sean said.

"I thought we would stay in today," Charlotte commented.

"Maybe, tonight, but today, we're going out."

The doorbell rang. "That's probably for you. I'll be right back," Charlotte said, before she could inquire more about Sean's plans.

Charlotte opened the door and Priscilla stood there dangling keys in one hand, suitcase in the other.

"So this is where you stay," Priscilla said with a snarl on her face. "Nice house," she remarked, as she handed Charlotte the keys. "Tell Sean, he owes me a bonus for this."

163

Charlotte took the suitcase from Priscilla. "Thanks for bringing these over."

"Sean's welcome."

"Priscilla, I'm not going anywhere. I'm here to stay so it's in both of our best interests we get along. So can you drop the attitude?"

Priscilla laughed. "I don't have an attitude. Maybe you need to check *your* attitude."

Priscilla left Charlotte staring at her as she got into the passenger side of a waiting truck. Priscilla waved at her as the truck pulled off. Sean's SUV was parked behind her car.

*She's a strange one,* Charlotte thought to herself. She closed the door and took the things to Sean.

"I heard everything. You have to forgive Priscilla. She sometimes acts like a mother hen. She doesn't mean anything by it."

"Why do you keep making excuses for her?" Charlotte asked.

"She's not always like that. You've seen her in action. She's usually polite and very professional," Sean said, as he unzipped the suitcase. He removed a pair of jeans and shirt. "Do you have an iron and iron board?" he asked.

"I sure do. While you're ironing, I'll go cook breakfast," Charlotte said.

Charlotte left the room. She returned with an iron and iron board. She plugged the iron into a nearby outlet. She looked at Sean. "Sean, I understand Priscilla's someone you've had around since you started off in this business, but if you want to go to the next level, you will need to get rid of her. She was supposed to tell you I was in Houston, but she didn't. What if she's kept other things from you that you should have known? Just something to think about."

Charlotte left Sean alone with his thoughts.

# Chapter Forty

Sean ironed his clothes and thought about what Charlotte said regarding Priscilla. Priscilla normally was nice, but this was about his business and he couldn't have her being rude to people. He made a mental note to speak with Priscilla later about her attitude. Maybe she was dealing with something but he would find out later. For now, he wanted to concentrate on Charlotte.

Sean dressed and followed the aroma of the food. Charlotte stood over the stove making an omelet.

"Anything you want me to do?" Sean asked.

"Just sit down and relax."

Sean sat at the table, pulled out his cell phone and surfed the internet. He snapped a photo of Charlotte cooking. He cropped the picture so Charlotte's face wouldn't be in it then posted it on his social media accounts with the caption, "There's nothing sexier than a woman cooking her man breakfast."

Within a matter of seconds, his social media platforms lit up. He laughed out loud at some of the comments.

"What's so funny?" Charlotte asked.

"Nothing. Just reading comments on this picture I just posted on Instagram."

Charlotte walked to the table and sat a plate in front of him. "I hope you like my omelet."

Sean licked his lips. "If it tastes as good as you, I'm going to love it."

"Get your mind out the gutter."

"You shouldn't be so sexy," Sean said.

He put his phone down. Charlotte picked it up before sitting down. He reached for it but she swatted his hand away. "Nope. I want to see this picture."

He waited for her response.

She looked at him. "Why did you post this? What happened to anonymity? You of all people know I cherish my privacy."

"Nobody knows it's you, but me. And you should be happy. Did you see the comments? The men agree."

Charlotte scrolled down on his phone and then handed it to him. "You're all perverts."

"I just caught your best ass-et. Men like me like big butts." Sean burst out with the "Sir-Mix-A-lot" song.

"You better eat your omelet before it gets cold. I forgot to get us some juice. Do you want orange juice or cranberry?" Charlotte asked.

"Cranberry works for me," Sean responded.

Charlotte went to the refrigerator and returned with a plastic bottle of Cranberry juice.

After breakfast, Sean made a few phone calls while Charlotte cleaned the kitchen. Charlotte plopped down on the couch beside him.

"I've decided to not work today so the day's yours," Charlotte said.

"Great. Grab your keys and let's get out of here."

"Do I need to change?" Charlotte asked.

"What you have on is fine," Sean responded.

"Are you sure?" Charlotte asked.

"Jeans and a t-shirt are perfect for where we're going."

Sean and Charlotte left and got into his SUV. He got on the freeway and drove. Charlotte said, after an hour. "Sean, where are you taking me? The city is the other way."

"Sit back and relax."

"It's hard to relax when you don't know where you're going," Charlotte said.

"We're almost there." Sean drove less than a mile and then turned on a dirt road.

A huge sign that read, "Cartwright's Ranch" hung near a fence.

"Welcome to the wild wild west," Sean said, as he turned off the air conditioner and let down the windows so the natural air could blow through the truck.

The ranch had plenty of cows and horses. Sean parked his SUV near several other vehicles.

Sean turned off the engine. "Have you ever ridden a horse before?"

"No. And I'm not about to ride one now," Charlotte muttered.

"Come on, baby, it's fun. I'll teach you."

Sean opened her door. Charlotte got out. "I'm not too sure about this. I'll watch you, if you want to ride."

They were greeted at the gate. "Sean, where you've been, man?" a stocky man wearing blue jeans, a blue jean shirt and a cowboy hat asked.

"Making music. What's up with you, Freddie?" Sean asked.

Freddie patted his stomach. "Eating, riding and drinking and in that order."

Freddie and Sean laughed.

Sean said, "I want you to meet my lady. Charlotte, this is Freddie. He lets me keep my horses here."

"You with this dude? You must don't know the things I know about him."

"Freddie, chill out. I had a hard time ringing this one in. You're going to make her bolt," Sean teased.

"Nice to meet you, Freddie. I think," Charlotte said, as she shook Freddie's hand.

"Come on in. Let me saddle two of them for you," Freddie responded.

"She's a virgin."

Charlotte hit Sean on the arm.

"I'm talking about riding horses, baby. Chill out."

"Oh," Charlotte responded.

Freddie laughed. "You have to excuse Sean. He doesn't know how to act around a lady. Now a fellow like me. I know how to treat a lady such as yourself."

"Oh you do. I might have me a new boyfriend when I leave this place."

Sean pouted. "Freddie, we are cool and all, but you better stop flirting with my woman."

They all laughed.

"Is there a restroom I can use?" Charlotte asked.

"Sure. Go through the door, down the hall and to your right. You can't miss it," Freddie responded.

"You got any boots in a size nine?" Sean asked, once Charlotte was gone.

"As a matter of fact, just got a new shipment of boots in. Might find some in your size too."

"How much will it cost me?"

"I'll add it to your bill."

"I think I would rather pay now." Sean laughed.

Sean followed Freddie inside. He watched as Freddie went through some boxes and handed two of them to him.

"The top one is her size and the bottom one, you should be able to fit."

"Thanks, man." Sean sat the boxes down.

"I'm going to go saddle them horses. I'll be waiting by the fence when you'll get ready."

Sean removed his tennis shoes.

"You're going to be a real cowboy for real with those boots," Charlotte said.

Sean pointed at the box near him. "I got you a pair too. Try them on."

Charlotte shook her hand out in front of her. "I told you I'm not getting on a horse."

Sean pled with his eyes. "Please. Just try it one time. If you don't like it, I promise never to ask you to go horseback riding ever again."

Charlotte sighed. "Okay. I'll try it."

"Great. I can't wait for you to ride my horse," Sean teased.

"I bet you can't."

"Now, whose mind is in the gutter?"

Charlotte smiled at him and put on her boots. "Been hanging around you too long I guess."

# Chapter Forty-One

Charlotte held on for dear life as the horse she was on decided to go full speed ahead. Sean rode his horse up beside her.

"Pull the left reign slightly. It'll slow her down," Sean said.

Charlotte did as instructed. The horse slowed down. Charlotte felt relieved. "I was enjoying it until she started to take off."

"When you kicked your foot, she thought you wanted to increase your speed. Every movement you make means something to the horse."

They rode the horses out to an open spring. Sean got off his horse and tied the horse to the tree. . He helped Charlotte get off her horse. They kissed briefly. Sean tied Charlotte's horse up next to his. They stood near the brink while the horses drank some of the water.

Charlotte looked out over the open land. "This is beautiful. How did you find out about this place?"

"One of my buddies from back home. When I lived in Houston, we used to go to the rodeos and trail rides. I've been riding horses since I was a little boy. I stopped riding for a while, but a friend of mine told me about the Cartwright Ranch. I checked it out. Liked the people. Found a few horses, bought some and brought them out here."

"Freddie is something else," Charlotte said.

"He means no harm. Ranching is all he knows."

"I wish I knew someone. I'm sure living out here could be lonely."

"Freddie's a millionaire. He has a house a few miles from here that will put my house to shame. If something happens to Freddie, his wife will be well taken care of."

"Wife?" Charlotte asked.

"Yes. Believe it or not, the old coot is married. If you get to meet his wife, Betty, you'll see they were made for each other. She'll have you laughing just as much as Freddie."

One of the horses started making a sound. They turned to look. "Is he alright?" Charlotte asked.

"Yes. But we do need to be making our way back towards the front. Are you thirsty?" Sean asked.

"I'm not drinking that water after those horses."

Sean laughed. "No, silly. We've both got flasks."

Sean walked to her horse and removed the flask from the side of the saddle. He handed it to her.

"After last night, I decided to slow down on the alcohol," Charlotte revealed.

"It's water. Trust me." Sean opened his flask and took a drink out of it. He held it to Charlotte's nose and said, "See. No alcohol."

Charlotte unfastened hers and drank the water. It quenched her thirst.

"Nothing like having your butt in my face," Sean said, after he finally got her on top of the saddle after the third try.

Charlotte said, "Sean, I'm glad you brought me out here. This was fun. It was different."

"I'm glad you're enjoying yourself."

They rode their horses back to the front.

Sean got off his horse. "Wait. I want to get a picture of you on the horse."

Sean removed his cell phone from his pocket and snapped a photo.

He helped Charlotte down. Charlotte took his phone. "I need to get you on top."

They took turns taking photos of one another.

They said their good-byes to Freddie and headed back to Los Angeles.

Sean reached across the seat. Charlotte held his hand. Verbal conversation wasn't needed between them. Being in each other's presence was enough. Charlotte enjoyed spending the day with Sean.

She'd never been horseback riding. They had pictures to mark their trip but she didn't need the pictures because she could vividly recall the time in her head.

She looked over at Sean. He seemed at peace. She smiled. She squeezed his hand.

"I love you," Sean said. He brought her hand up to his mouth and kissed the back of it.

"I love you too," Charlotte responded.

Traffic increased the closer they got back to the city limits. The green sign saying Los Angeles County greeted them.

Some rude person blew their horn when passing by them.

"I guess I was going too slow," Sean said.

Charlotte leaned over and looked at the speedometer. "You're going seventy-five."

"I know. Crazy, isn't it?"

"Some people don't need driver's licenses," Charlotte said, as she leaned back in her seat.

"You got that right." Sean agreed.

Before long, they were back at Charlotte's place.

Charlotte went to her kitchen, looked in the freezer and didn't see anything she could thaw out quick to cook. She walked back in the living room. Sean sat on the sofa flipping through the television stations.

"Let's make this a pizza night," Charlotte said.

"You get no arguments from me."

Charlotte ordered a pizza with everything on it and a couple of cans of soda. "Someone should be here in forty-five minutes."

Sean looked at his watch. "The countdown is on."

The pizza arrived. They ate, talked, watched movies and made love into the morning light.

The next day, they lounged around Charlotte's house talking with one another. The bond between the two of them tightened.

"Promise me, you won't let anything come between us ever again," Sean said.

Charlotte looped her fingers through Sean's as she laid on his chest. "I won't. Our past is our past and will not have a place in our relationship."

"Exactly." Sean kissed Charlotte on the top of her head.

"Sean, one day I will be ready to share what we have with the world, but for now, thank you for keeping our relationship a secret."

"People know I'm involved with someone but they just don't know who," Sean affirmed.

"Let's keep it that way."

"You don't have to worry about me saying a word," Sean said. "It'll be our own little secret."

Charlotte leaned forward and right before kissing him said, "I love you."

# Chapter Forty-Two

Sean woke up Monday morning feeling like a new man. He'd just spent a wonderful weekend with the woman he loved. He wanted to tell the world how he felt but he'd promised Charlotte he would keep her identity a secret.

He originally fell in love with the image of Charlotte, but after getting to know her on a more personal level, Sean was in love with the woman inside of her. The one she rarely showed to the outside world. He understood her need to exert control, but when she was around him, she could relinquish that control. She didn't have to make all of the decisions. She could be carefree and that's how he wanted her to be. He wanted her to feel free to be her complete self around him.

Some men couldn't deal with an independent woman. Sean found it exhilarating. It turned him on to see Charlotte at work. He liked how she maneuvered through bad situations and how she resolved problems that would make the average person crumble. Charlotte liked being in control but she knew when to allow Sean to take the wheel. He would never deny Charlotte and this weekend sealed it for him. Now that she's allowed him into her heart without any reservations, he would do whatever it took to protect her heart.

He pulled his SUV up in front of his house. Priscilla greeted him at the door.

"I was beginning to think you got lost," Priscilla said, as she moved out of the way and let him in.

"Last time I checked, I was a grown man. I don't have to check in with anyone."

Priscilla held her phone in the air. "I'm your assistant. I should know where you are at all times, in case you're needed."

"You knew where I was."

"I'm assuming you were with that woman, but I don't know for sure," Priscilla snapped.

"That woman's name is Charlotte. And if you're going to be around me, you will respect her."

"She's not right for you," Priscilla groaned.

Sean stopped walking. He turned around and looked at Priscilla. "You need to check your attitude."

"I'm serious, Sean. I tried to tell you what she did to Big Boss. Do you want her to ruin your career too?"

"Either you respect my relationship with Charlotte or you can bounce?"

Priscilla's lower lip started shaking. "Are you firing me?"

Sean tried his best not to fire her. "Why don't you take some time off? Clear your head. Get yourself together."

Priscilla clenched her teeth. "I can't believe you're firing me."

"I wasn't going to fire you, but since you don't want to take a few days off to cool down like I suggested, you've left me no choice."

"What am I supposed to do about money? How am I supposed to maintain my lifestyle? I can't believe you're firing me." Priscilla went on and on.

Sean walked near her. "I will give you a monthly allowance until you find something else."

"The economy is bad. What if it takes me a year?" she asked.

"I got you. I'm not going to let you starve."

"We're family. Isn't that what you like to say?" She mimicked his voice when she said, "We're family."

"Priscilla, my decision to release you from your duties is business, not personal."

Priscilla backed up some. She inhaled and exhaled loudly. "Won't nobody have your back like I've had your back. Believe that." Priscilla stormed out the house, slamming the front door.

The mirror on the wall shook.

Sean opened the front door and watched Priscilla screech out of the driveway. He got his phone out and called Trevon. "I need every lock in my house changed ASAP," Sean commanded.

"Was there a burglary?" Trevon asked from the other end of the phone.

"No. I had to fire my assistant."

"I'll send someone out to change the locks right away," Trevon responded. "If I were you, I would also change all of my passwords."

"Thanks. I will do that," Sean said. He disconnected the call and went straight to his home office and sat behind his computer. He opened his drawer and pulled out a list of all of the websites and login information. He changed the password to each one of them. He also changed the passwords to his bank account and email addresses.

Sean made a few phone calls. "Bobby, this is Sean. I just fired Priscilla," Sean said.

Bobby cursed from the other end of the phone. "Man, I hope you're ready to deal with the wrath of a crazy woman."

"We're good. I just wanted you to know. I'm going to hire someone but not sure how long it will take. In the meantime, I might need you to take up some slack."

"I got you," Bobby responded. "Oops. That's her on my other line. I'm not answering. She can get voice mail."

"You don't have to avoid her on my account," Sean said.

Sean called his sister, Marie, in Houston and told her what happened. "It's something that had to be done. You couldn't keep her around if she's being rude to people. She's a reflection of you. She'll be fine. If she wants to come back to Houston, I'll let her stay here until she can get settled."

"Great. Call and let her know. I'm sure she'll appreciate it," Sean said. He felt better about his decision after talking to Marie.

# Chapter Forty-Three

A smile seemed to be glued to Charlotte's face the entire day. Even though, this Monday was like any other hectic Monday, Charlotte refused to let anything get under her skin. She went about her normal Monday activities without a care in the world.

Felicia called her on the phone. "Sean's on the phone. He said he's been trying to reach you on your cell."

"I still have it on silent. Didn't want the ringer interrupting my conference call. Put him through."

"Hi, Sean, how are you?" Charlotte asked.

Charlotte picked up her cell phone and saw she had several missed calls from Sean and two text messages asking her to call him.

"I fired Priscilla. I'm in desperate need for an assistant. Do you know of anyone?" Sean blurted.

"Wow. I wasn't expecting to hear that," Charlotte said.

Charlotte listened to Sean recap his Monday morning events. While she was basking in the afterglow of their weekend, Sean was dealing with Godzilla who went by the name of Priscilla.

"Baby, don't worry about a thing. By the end of the day, we will have you a new assistant. I will have the candidates come here. Felicia can narrow them down to three and you can interview them right here at my office," Charlotte said.

"Thanks, Babe. You're a life saver. What time?"

"Six. She needs enough time to decide on which candidates will be the best."

"I will be there around six."

"Did you change all of your passwords...the locks on your doors?" Charlotte asked.

"Done."

"Good. Try not to be upset."

"She's been my right hand for a long time. I feel lost without her already."

"Know this, Sean. You can lean on me. I've got your back."

"She was well organized. She kept things running smoothly."

"Those are qualities your next assistant will have. So as I said, I've got you covered. Relax."

"I'll try. I know you've got work to do, so I'll go so you can get back to it," Sean said.

Charlotte called Felicia. "Can you come to my office? I need your assistance with something."

An hour later, Felicia informed Charlotte that the interviews had been scheduled.

"Have a seat. I want to talk to you about something."

Felicia took a seat in front of Charlotte's desk and crossed her legs.

Charlotte slid a manila folder in front of Felicia. "You've been going beyond the call of duty, not just for me, or the other associates, but our clients. How does a promotion sound with a substantial raise?"

Felicia opened the folder and reviewed the sheet of paper inside it. Her mouth flew open. "Office manager and I would be making fifteen thousand dollars more a year than what I'm making now. Where do I sign?"

Charlotte held up her pen. "Here you go."

Felicia signed the paper. "Where's my new office?"

"For now, I still need you at the front desk. I want you to hire your replacement and train her. I will leave the time frame to make this happen up to you."

Felicia stood and walked behind the desk and gave Charlotte a tight hug.

"I love you, girl. Thank you for believing in me. I know sometimes I can get in your business but that's only because I care about you. I have five brothers and you're like the sister I never had."

Charlotte patted Felicia on the arm and tried to break the embrace. "Alright. It's good. Now let's get back to me being the boss and you handling your business."

Felicia stood. "You try to act like you're Ms. Cool all of the time, but I know the real you. You're a softy underneath that tough exterior."

"Bye, Felicia." Charlotte laughed.

"I'm going. I can't wait to tell my friends. They are going to be so envious."

Felicia practically skipped out of the room. Charlotte smiled, knowing business was so good she was able to give one of her hardest working employees a promotion.

At six o'clock, Charlotte sat in on the interviews with Sean. The first two candidates didn't seem to be a match. "Felicia, send in the last candidate," Charlotte said, over the intercom.

"I hope this one is better. I really need to find an assistant," Sean uttered.

Charlotte and Sean both seemed to be surprised that the last candidate was a male. Charlotte had assumed Taylor was a woman. She'd gone to school with several girls named Taylor.

Charlotte and Sean stood and extended their hand out and Taylor shook it. Taylor was twenty-two years old and a recent graduate from the University of California with a Bachelor's Degree in business.

They each took turns asking Taylor questions. Sean said, "You are aware if I choose you to be my assistant, that you will not have a typical forty hour week. I will be going on a world tour in a few months. You will be required to travel with me when I go out of town unless it's a personal trip."

"I'm not married nor do I have any kids. I want to work in the entertainment field. I feel being your assistant will give me hands on training. I also feel some of the things I learned in school can also be beneficial to you. I know you have a strong social media presence and I want to help continue to build your brand using that resource. I also know that you have certain organizations you support financially and also with your time," Taylor said.

Sean looked at Charlotte. Sean looked at Taylor. "Can you wait outside for a few minutes?"

Once the door was closed, Sean asked Charlotte, "What do you think?"

Charlotte paused. "I sort of hate Felicia chose him for you because I could use him in my office."

"So you think I should give him a try then too?" Sean asked.

"Yes. If you don't hire him, I will."

Sean got up and opened the door. "Taylor, can you come back in?"

Taylor walked in.

"Taylor, I want to offer you the job." Sean extended his hand.

Taylor shook his hand. "Thank you. I'm very appreciative of this opportunity."

Charlotte stood and shook his hand. "Let me get Felicia. She'll go over everything with you. You will need to sign confidentiality agreements, payroll, etcetera. Welcome to Team Sean Maxwell."

# Chapter Forty-Four

Sean sat in his living room with his new assistant later on that night. He handed Taylor a bag.

Taylor removed a new iPhone and iPad from the bag.

"These are for you. Protective cases and everything else you need are at the bottom of the bag."

"Mr. Maxwell, thank you again for this opportunity."

"Taylor, call me Sean. Charlotte had Felicia retrieve my itinerary and printed it out. This is what I have going on this month and she printed out the last previous months to give you an idea of what to expect. I'm going to be depending on you to handle day-to-day activities for me. As you mentioned during the interview, social media is very important to my brand." Sean went to his desk. He picked up a sheet of paper and handed it to Taylor. "This is a list of all of the websites and login information. If you can't read my handwriting let me know."

Taylor looked at the paper. "It looks fine to me."

"Great. Do me a favor. Type it up and get me a printed copy of it so I can keep for my records. One thing I ask, if you change the password due to someone trying to hack, always let me know what the new password is. You never know when I'm going to access any one of my pages. I use my Instagram a lot. I have it set to repost on my Facebook and Twitter pages so it's important you keep me informed."

"Yes, sir."

Sean said, "You will also be working closely with Jason Lewis. He's a member of Charlotte's agency. You've already met Felicia. You will hear from her from time to time. First order of business for you tomorrow morning is to order the biggest bouquets of flowers and have them sent to Felicia and Charlotte. You'll find their information on the iPad."

Taylor took notes on his notepad.

"Do you have any questions for me?" Sean asked.

"Yes. What happened to your last assistant?" Taylor asked.

"She didn't play well with others and if you're working for me, that's unacceptable. I will not tolerate the mistreatment of others in my camp." Sean looked at Taylor and didn't blink.

"I try to treat people the same. My mom said we're all God's children and no one person is better than the other," Taylor said.

"Good. I'm glad we have an understanding on what my expectations are."

"What time should I be here tomorrow?" Taylor asked.

"Get here around nine. I should be through with my morning workout by then."

Sean walked Taylor to the door. "Once we both see how this works out for us, I will probably give you a key and the alarm code so you can come and go as you please."

"I understand."

Taylor left and Sean went upstairs to his room to call Charlotte. "I need to see you."

"I can't. I had a client emergency and I'm on my way to their house now to deal with it," Charlotte responded.

"Call me when you get a free moment," Sean said, a little disappointed that he wouldn't be seeing Charlotte later on.

"It will probably be late, so I'll call you tomorrow."

"You want me waiting up all night worrying about you?" Sean asked.

"I'll text you when I make it back home. I'm warning you now, it'll be late."

"I don't care how late it is. I won't rest until I know you're safely back at home," Sean said.

Sean needed to get a grip on his emotions. He hoped he didn't come across as some over protective possessive boyfriend. He cared about Charlotte and didn't want anything to happen to her. He knew she was used to taking care of herself, but she had him now. He wanted to be her protector and be there for her when she needed him.

Sean's phone rang interrupting his thoughts. He answered.

"Sean, it's me. Priscilla."

"Have you calmed down?" he asked.

"Yes. I just wanted to apologize for my behavior earlier," Priscilla said.

"I want you to know there aren't any hard feelings. You can still come to me if you need me," Sean tried to assure her.

"I need my job back," Priscilla pleaded.

"It's too late for that." Sean remained on the phone and headed to his home gym.

"But, what am I supposed to do, Sean?" Priscilla asked.

"You have so many good qualities that it will be easy for you to find another job. Let me know what day you want to fly to Houston. I'll pay for the ticket and your hotel."

"Sean, I've been thinking. Houston no longer feels like home to me. I want to stay right here."

"Cool. Then, get your resume together. I'll give you a glowing recommendation."

"But, I liked working for you. I don't want to work for anyone else."

"Priscilla, I don't feel like getting into this with you. I've made my decision and it's final. As I said earlier, I'm still here for you, but we can't work together."

"Fine."

Sean looked at his phone and saw that Priscilla disconnected the call.

He put on his workout gear. He needed to release some of the built-up frustrations.

# Chapter Forty-Five

"Stop already," Charlotte shouted out loud as her alarm beeped several times. With her eyes barely opened, Charlotte reached over and hit the snooze button for the second time. She didn't get home until after two and the clock beside her bed read six thirty in the morning. She needed to get up because she needed to meet with Raquel, an actress in her twenties with a drug addiction problem. Raquel's reckless behavior was now affecting her career. She got fired yesterday for coming on the set high. Charlotte's job was to prepare Raquel for an interview with one of the networks.

Charlotte moved in slow motion but got dressed and out of the house in time. On the way to her client's house, she called Felicia.

"Reschedule my morning appointments. I'm going to help get Raquel out of this mess, but after this, she will need to find someone else to represent her. I can't help someone who doesn't want to help themselves."

"Calm down. You said that the last time, remember," Felicia reminded her.

"But I mean it this time. This is it. She's too old for this. Get the rehab set up and I'll be dropping her off at the facility right after this interview."

Charlotte's phone beeped. She saw the number display on car's console. "Let me get this call. I'll call you when we leave Raquel's house."

Charlotte clicked the button to switch to the other call. She blurted out, "I was going to call you."

Sean responded, "Can you do lunch today?"

"I wish. Remember the problem I went to resolve last night? Well, it's moved over into today. I won't be back in the office until after lunch."

"You have to eat sometime. Let's meet for a late lunch."

"Sean, I'm not trying to blow you off, but today, I really can't."

Charlotte talked to Sean until she made it to Raquel's house. "Baby, I've got to go. I'm here and I see the paparazzi is too," Charlotte said, as she honked her horn to alert the paparazzi to move out of her way as she drove up the driveway to Raquel's house.

"This is going to be a long day," Charlotte said, right before getting out of her car to face the mess her client caused.

Later on that night, Charlotte lay on her stomach enjoying the feel of Sean's hands.

Sean kissed the top of her back. "I told you I give good massages."

"You're supposed to be rubbing," Charlotte said, as she turned her head to the side and closed her eyes.

"Like this?" Sean asked.

"Yes. I like that," Charlotte responded.

Sean continued to massage the small of her back. His hand lowered. He began massaging her buttocks with both of his hands. "You can't get this type of treatment at the spa."

He replaced his hands with his lips. Charlotte squirmed. "Sean, come on now. You're supposed to be massaging my full body. You haven't even made it to my legs yet."

"Oh yes. The legs. Just wait until I get to those body parts."

Charlotte smiled. She was enjoying the feel of Sean's hands and the softness of his lips when they touched her body. It didn't take long for her full body massage to turn into them making love. Charlotte cried out his name and fell on top of him. Their bodies were drenched down in sweat. "Now, I don't feel guilty about not working out today," Charlotte said.

Sean grinned. "That was just the appetizer. Are you ready for the main course?"

"What am I going to do with you?" Charlotte asked.

Sean shifted in the bed where they were now side by side looking each other. "Love me and let me love you."

Charlotte looked at him as she spoke. "You know I love you. There shouldn't be any doubt about that."

"I don't doubt your love. I just want to make sure you and I are on the same page. I don't want there to be any misunderstandings between us," Sean said.

Charlotte touched Sean's face. "You've been nothing but kind to me. You put up with my demands and I'm grateful. I love you, Sean Maxwell, and there's nothing you or anyone else can do about it."

Charlotte leaned forward and kissed him. She gently pushed him down on his back. She continued to kiss him as she positioned herself on top of him.

Charlotte stopped kissing him and sat on top of him and began bouncing up and down and rotating her hips. Sean reached his hand forward and rubbed her nipples.

"Ooh, baby," Sean moaned over and over.

Charlotte swung her hair from side to side, as she rode Sean like he was a thoroughbred horse. Sean grabbed her by her hips. Her pace increased. Her movements seemed to be driving Sean over the edge. The more she moved, the louder Sean's moans got. Charlotte could feel herself coming close to the brink of an orgasm.

She leaned down and covered Sean's mouth with hers. Sean held her tight as they came to a climax together.

## Chapter Forty-Six

The next morning over breakfast, Charlotte asked Sean, "How's your new assistant working out?"

"So far, so good," Sean responded, while pouring himself some orange juice.

Charlotte rubbed her foot up and down Sean's leg under the table. "Thank you for the massage. It was just what I needed."

"I'm here to please." Sean licked his lips.

"Don't do that," Charlotte said.

"You mean this." Sean licked his lips again.

Charlotte tightened the belt of her robe. "Sean, I'm not playing with you. I don't have time to fool with you this morning. I have several stops to make before going into the office."

"Speaking of office. Did you get the flowers I sent?"

"Yes, babe." She got up and wrapped her arm around his neck and kissed him on the cheek. "They were beautiful. So much stuff was happening that I forgot to tell you."

"No problem. Just wanted to make sure you got them."

"I did. They're lovely. You're spoiling me with the flowers."

"If you moved in with me, I could spoil you even more."

Charlotte released her arms and leaned over him to get his empty plate. "I'm not sure about that. I've tried the living together thing before. It didn't work out."

"There you go bringing your past into our relationship," Sean said, but regretted it as soon as it came out of his mouth.

"Am I supposed to repeat previous mistakes? No. I learn from them and try to do better going forward." Charlotte placed the dirty dishes in the dishwasher.

"You're right. I'm wrong for even saying it." Sean stood and walked behind Charlotte.

She moved away. "I really don't have time. I'm already leaving later than I'd planned on."

Sean threw both of his hands up. "I get it. I'll leave you alone so you can get dressed. While you're doing that, I'll finish cleaning."

Charlotte walked up to him and kissed him. "Thank you, baby. You're a sweetheart."

"No kissing. Don't want to start something you can't finish," Sean pouted.

"I'll make it up to you," Charlotte said, as she walked away.

"I'm going to hold you to that promise." Sean washed the pan and tray she used to cook their breakfast on.

He used Charlotte's spare bathroom to shower. She was fully dressed by the time he walked into her bedroom with nothing but a towel wrapped around his waist.

Charlotte whistled. "I might have to reconsider your offer. I can see myself coming home to this every night."

"Don't play with me like that. I'm serious about you moving in," Sean said. He took out a pair of boxers, jogging pants and shirt from his gym bag.

He removed the towel giving Charlotte a clear view of his naked behind.

"I'll think about it. That's the best I can do for now," Charlotte countered.

Sean put on his boxers. He turned around to face her. "I'll take that for now."

Charlotte handed him a key. "I have to go. Lock up when you leave. My alarm code is 9168."

They kissed and Charlotte left him alone. He placed the key on the nightstand and continued to get dressed.

When Sean arrived home, he saw what appeared to be two people in a heated discussion outside of his front door. He rushed and parked.

"What's going on here?" he asked.

Priscilla spoke first. "He won't let me into your house. He says, I'm not on the list. How come I'm not on the list, Sean?"

"Mr. Maxwell, I mean, Sean, I was only doing my job. You instructed me to only allow people on the list inside when you're not around," Taylor said.

Sean looked at Taylor. "You did good. Go inside. I'll take care of her." Sean grabbed Priscilla by the arm in an attempt to lead her towards her car.

She jerked her arm away. "I tried using my key but it didn't work. I can't believe you. You changed the locks on me. What's wrong, Sean? Do you not trust me anymore?" Priscilla crossed her arms, tapped her foot and looked at him.

Sean ignored her questions. "What are you doing here?" he asked.

"I came to talk to you about getting my job back but I see you've already replaced me."

"You can never be replaced. But as I told you over the phone, you and I can't work together any more. You must move on." Sean tried to remain calm but Priscilla was trying his patience.

Priscilla started laughing. "This has got to be a joke. You're punking me for that TV show aren't you. Okay. It's funny. Ha ha. Now come on, Sean."

Sean grabbed Priscilla by the arm and practically dragged her to her car. He opened the door. "Bye, Priscilla. I think it's best you don't come around here anymore. I will have Taylor pack any belongings you may have left behind in the office and ship them to you. But as of this moment, you are no longer welcomed on the premises."

Priscilla poked her lips out. "I'm sorry okay."

"Bye, Priscilla," Sean said. He folded his arms and watched her speed away.

Taylor waited near the front door.

Sean walked inside and closed the door. "I'm glad you didn't allow her into the house."

"She's crazy," Taylor concluded.

"She's upset because I fired her."

"So that's why she kept yelling about not being replaced? For a moment I thought she was a crazy ex-girlfriend."

"I've dated some crazy women in my time, but Priscilla wasn't one of them," Sean said, as he walked off with Taylor fast on his heels.

## Chapter Forty-Seven

The next few weeks, Sean balanced his schedule between writing new songs and taking additional acting lessons from Rose. Taylor was working out as his assistant. Things between him and Charlotte were going well; except he still hadn't convinced her to move in with him.

They were seated on his couch. He had her feet in his hands massaging them. "What do I have to do to convince you that it's time for us to take this relationship to another level?"

"I think things are perfect just the way they are." Charlotte leaned her head back and enjoyed her massage.

"I want to wake up with you. I want to hold you through the night. I want to smell your essence as I fall asleep."

"That sounds like a song. You should write it," Charlotte teased.

"I'm serious. Charlotte, it will save us both time. Either I have to drive to your side of town or you have to drive here. Living together will be convenient."

Charlotte moved her feet and crawled and got on top of Sean. "You're making some valid points. But you keep forgetting, we're supposed to keep our relationship a secret. If we move in together, that's going to be impossible."

"I'm ready to come out. Come out to the world and let them know I'm with the most wonderful woman in the world," Sean said.

"Knowing you feel that way is enough for me. I'm not one of those women who need to stake claim to her man in public. I know what we have. I know regardless of what I read in the news or on one of those gossip blogs, you're committed to me." Charlotte kissed him.

They heard someone walk in the room and clear their throat. Charlotte jumped off the couch. She rubbed her hands down her pants.

Sean sat up. "Taylor, I thought you were gone for today."

"I'm sorry. I forgot my iPad. I hadn't synced it with my phone today and didn't want to forget any tasks."

Charlotte looked at Sean and then at Taylor. "We might as well tell him."

Sean said, "Taylor, you know Charlotte right?"

"Yes. She's here a lot."

"As I'm sure you've figured out, she's more than just my manager."

Taylor waved his hand out in front of him. "Sean, whatever you do is your business. I'm not one to judge."

Sean laughed. "Charlotte's someone special to me. She's my lady. I'm committed to her. If it was up to me, she would be living here." Sean looked at Charlotte.

Taylor rubbed his hand on his pants. Sean could tell he was nervous.

Charlotte added, "What Sean is trying to say is that, we're a couple; however we don't want the public to know it. So we would like for you to keep it under wraps."

Sean said, "Yes. Please don't let anyone else know. Even if they ask, just direct them to me for a response."

"Or me," Charlotte added.

"Oh okay. People online are curious about who you're dating. Especially after some of your Instagram photos."

Charlotte looked at Sean. "Have you been posting pictures of me on Instagram that I don't know about?"

"Guilty as charged. That big butt of yours is famous, baby." Sean laughed.

"Taylor, unless you want to be a witness to murder, I suggest you get your iPad and get out of here now because Sean's about to get it." Charlotte removed a pillow off the couch and hit him with it.

Sean picked up the pillow off the floor and they were involved in a pillow fight.

Taylor left the room.

They ended on the sofa with Sean on top of Charlotte. "I bet you he thinks we're crazy," Charlotte said.

"He's all business all the time. I'm trying to get him to loosen up a little," Sean said.

"Just give him some time. He's trying to feel you out. He takes his job seriously."

"Enough talk about Taylor. I want to get back to our conversation."

"You mean the one where you were telling me how special I am and how I make your world brighter and your toes curl." Charlotte's smile widened.

"No, it was the one where you told me you were going to consider moving in with me because you can't stand sleeping in an empty bed."

Charlotte wrapped her arm around Sean's neck. "You make it so hard to say no."

"Then say, yes." Sean pouted.

"All I can say is I'll think about it."

"But you keep telling me that." Sean tilted his head to the side and frowned.

"I'll give you a definite answer soon. I promise," Charlotte said, right before kissing Sean.

Sean knew she was trying to distract him from the question. He wouldn't press further…for now at least. Instead, he enjoyed the feel of her soft lips.

# Chapter Forty-Eight

"Sean, I've got to go," Charlotte said the next morning. It was after eight o'clock. She'd overslept and forgot to bring a change of clothes. She had a luncheon to speak at so she had to rush home to get dressed.

"I'll walk you out," Sean said, as he rubbed his eyes.

"No need to. I'll lock the bottom lock. Call you later." Charlotte gave Sean a quick peck on the lips. She grabbed her purse and keys from downstairs and hurried out the door. She had to stop in her tracks when something blinded her. She placed her hand over her face but didn't see anything. She continued to her car and sped off towards her house.

Two hours later, she stood behind a podium and addressed fifty women in the entertainment industry about women in Hollywood.

"As women, we have to be more aggressive to get what we want. When we are more aggressive, they call us the word we hate to be called."

One of the women in the audience said it for Charlotte.

Charlotte spoke for another fifteen minutes. She ended her speech by saying, "We mustn't let others forget our roles in Hollywood aren't limited to the screen. That we're not just pretty faces. Yes, we are skilled actors, we're writers, we're producers, we're agents, we're stuntwomen and we're whoever we want to be."

The women gave Charlotte a standing ovation.

Charlotte smiled and women gathered around her wanting to take pictures and ask her a few questions.

Mona and Kem waited until the crowd died down and approached her.

Mona and Kem gave her a hug.

Kem said, "You did great. You got me motivated to write another sitcom."

Charlotte smiled. "I know it'll be a winner too if you do."

"I'm so proud of you," Mona chided.

"Mona, your time is coming. Just don't give up," Charlotte assured her.

"I know. But today's not about me. It's about you, my friend. You deserve all the accolades you've gotten here today." Mona held Charlotte's award.

Charlotte took it from Mona and posed. Kem took the picture.

"I'll text it to both of you," Kem said.

"Great. Well, ladies, I still have work to do. Thank you for coming," Charlotte said.

"We wouldn't have missed this," Kem declared.

"I've got to get back to my cranky boss," Mona groaned.

Charlotte parted ways with her friends and drove straight to her office. She smiled when she saw a fresh bouquet of flowers on her desk. She closed her eyes and sniffed them. She removed the card from the plastic stem. She sat behind her desk and opened it. Her smile turned to a frown when she saw who the flowers were from.

She dialed Felicia's number. "Can you come to my office?"

A few minutes later, Felicia walked in.

"Can you remove these? In fact, donate them to the hospital down the street. Anything, just get them out of here."

"But they are so beautiful."

"If you won't do it, I will." Charlotte stood and picked up the flowers.

"I got it. Who are they from?" Felicia took them from her.

"You didn't look at the card?" Charlotte had a puzzled look on her face.

"They must have come in when I was out for lunch. I didn't even know they were on your desk."

"Remember, Darryl?"

"Yes, I remember you telling me about the jerk."

"His name is on the card. I don't want anything he's sending. If he calls, do not pass his call through."

Charlotte's phone rang. "Hello."

"A voice like an angel," a male voice said from the other end.

"Hold on." Charlotte looked at Felicia. "Please take them. Trash them, whatever."

"I've got this." Felicia left the room with the bouquet of flowers.

Charlotte took the phone off hold. "Thanks for holding."

"I see you haven't changed."

"Who is this?" Charlotte sat back down behind her desk.

"You're not going to thank me for the flowers. How rude?" Darryl laughed and then abruptly stopped.

"Why are you calling me?"

"I've missed you. I'll be in town for the Music Video Awards and wanted to see if we could get together and have dinner."

"Darryl, let's not pretend we're old friends. You've been to LA countless times but haven't tried to reach out to me before. So what makes this trip different?"

"I'm trying to make amends with those I've wronged. Aren't you going to allow me to do that?" he asked.

"I forgive you. So you can take me off the list and go call someone else that you need to apologize to."

"Still feisty. Just the way I remembered you."

"Look. I have a business to run so I don't have all evening to talk with you. Is there another reason for your call?" Charlotte asked.

"No, that was it. Thank you for forgiving me. And I forgive you too."

"Surely, you're delusional because I never did anything to you."

"You broke my heart. And for some, that's unforgiveable."

"Bye, Darryl. You're still full of it."

Charlotte hung up the phone. Her nerves were a little rattled. He was the last person she expected to hear from. It had been five years and unfortunately, he still had some affect over her.

Charlotte attempted to concentrate on her work, but hearing from Darryl brought back old bitter memories. It reminded her of a time when she was young, naive and trusting. Trusting Darryl almost ruined her.

Hours had passed and Charlotte hadn't finished anything on her to-do list. She turned off her computer, grabbed her purse and keys and left the office. She drove around with no destination in sight. She needed to clear her head.

Sean attempted to reach Charlotte by calling and texting her. He'd gotten no responses. He'd contacted Felicia to see if Charlotte had any events scheduled she knew about. She confirmed that the only event she had was the luncheon from earlier.

It was now after eight o'clock. This time after not getting a response, Sean hopped in his SUV and drove directly to her place.

He felt relieved when he saw her car parked in front of her house. He rang the doorbell and didn't get a response. He banged on the door.

Charlotte opened the door. "Sean, what's your problem? I was in the bathroom. I was coming."

"Is everything okay?" Sean asked. His eyes scanned over her body.

She was wearing a pair of sweat pants and a tank top. Physically she looked fine.

"Yes. I just needed some alone time."

"You could have sent a quick text saying that," Sean said.

They walked to the living room. "I didn't realize I needed to check in with you or anyone else."

"You saw my texts. So it would have been the right thing to do." Sean tried to control his temper. Charlotte's actions were grating on his nerves. She sat on the couch. She crossed her legs up under her. Sean sat near her.

"I'm not in the mood to argue with you," Charlotte whined.

"I drove all the way over here to check on you and you're the one with the attitude?"

"Look at me. I'm fine. So now you can ease your conscience and hop back in your truck and go back to your side of town. Charlotte is fine. Believe that."

Sean looked at Charlotte. He wasn't going anywhere. "This attitude of yours has nothing to do with me. What happened today to put you in a foul mood? I don't want to hear, 'nothing' either."

Charlotte moved her legs and placed them on the floor. "I really don't want to talk about it."

Sean scooted closer to Charlotte. He picked up her hand and held it. "We promised to communicate with one another. If you don't tell me what's wrong, I won't know how to help you fix the problem."

"Darryl's my problem. Okay, are you satisfied?" Charlotte hopped up off the couch. She stood in front of the television and walked back and forth.

Charlotte shared with him the conversation she had with Darryl.

"Baby, he didn't say anything out of order. He called to apologize. I don't understand why you're acting like this," Sean said.

"Because I don't trust him. It's been five years since we've talked. If we're at the same event, it's like we both go the opposite way to avoid one another. Why after five years is he reaching out and trying to be all friendly? No, he's up to something and I don't know what it is. I've worked too hard for him or anyone else to interfere."

Sean got up and walked over to Charlotte and wrapped his arm around her waist to stop her from walking. "Calm down. You've got me now. If he tries to do anything to harm you, I will take care of him personally."

"I'm so used to taking care of everything myself. I'm glad I have you." Charlotte squeezed him tight.

# Chapter Forty-Nine

Sean convinced Charlotte to go with him to the MVA. He'd also given her extra tickets so she invited Jason, Felicia, Mona and Kem. Charlotte brought her dress with her to the office because she knew she wouldn't have time to drive home, shower and change. She tuned in to a jazz station, relaxed a little prior to getting ready. Time flew by and before long it was time for her to get ready. She closed and locked her office door and got dressed.

Charlotte looked at the full-length mirror and was satisfied with her look. The exquisite black knee length evening gown revealed her cleavage. The sequined pattern wrapped around the waist area. The bottom of the evening gown flared out and was decorated with glittering accents on chiffon material. She wore three inch sequined heels.

Felicia knocked on the door and yelled from the other end. "The car's downstairs."

"I'm coming." Charlotte locked her big handbag in her bottom drawer of her desk. She picked her small black clutch purse and phone. She locked her office door and went to meet Felicia and Jason in the lobby.

"Don't you look beautiful," Charlotte said to Felicia.

Felicia wore a long red fitted halter dress. "Thanks and so do you. Looking like Cinderella."

"Let's hope the clock doesn't strike twelve because I sure don't want to turn into a pumpkin," Charlotte joked.

Jason cleared his throat. "I'm waiting."

"You look good too. But you didn't need either one of us to tell you that."

Charlotte loved picking on Jason.

"I know. I just like hearing it." Jason laughed.

A few minutes later, they were seated in the back of the limousine eating *hors d'oeuvres* and drinking champagne.

"When Sean said he was sending a car over, I didn't know he was providing us food too," Felicia said.

"He can be thoughtful," Charlotte acknowledged.

They ate while en route to the theater. Charlotte received a text message from Mona to inform her they would meet them there.

"Look at all the people," Jason noted.

"Sean wants us to walk the red carpet with him. It's going to get hectic but remember, we need to stay close together."

"I can't believe it. My first red carpet," Felicia said, attempting to hold back her excitement.

The driver opened the partition window. "Mr. Sean Maxwell is behind us."

Charlotte looked at Jason and Felicia. "Y'all ready?"

Jason looked at Felicia. "Smile. People will be taking your picture because they think you're famous. Don't worry that you're not. Just act like it."

Felicia smiled.

The driver opened the door. Jason got out first. He held his hand out. Felicia exited the limousine next. Charlotte gripped her handbag and carefully exited the limousine.

She looked towards the back of the limousine. Sean, in his signature all black designer suit, looked as if he could have walked off the pages of GQ Magazine. The cameras loved him. Everyone wanted to snap a picture of him and wanted to interview him.

Charlotte and Sean's eyes locked. He walked through the crowd of camera operators and over to where Charlotte, Felicia and Jason stood. He hugged Felicia first and shook Jason's hand. He hugged Charlotte and whispered in her ear, "You look stunning."

Charlotte blushed.

"Come on, let's go. The show will be starting soon," Sean said.

One of Sean's bodyguards helped lead the way. Charlotte walked a few inches behind Sean. Sean insisted that they all get in the picture during some of his photo opportunities. His hand seemed to find itself wrapped around Charlotte's waist.

Charlotte smiled and posed for more pictures than she cared for. Her phone vibrated. The text alerted her that Mona and Kem were also on the red carpet. Some of the entertainment reporters knew Kem, so they were trying to get her to share the scoop on some of her shows.

The ushers guided them to their seats. "These are good seats," Felicia remarked.

"I'm sitting on the end because I have to perform and present," Sean said. "Of course, you all know who's sitting next to me."

They all grinned and took their seats.

Sean leaned over and whispered in her ear, "I can't wait to get you home tonight."

"Sean." Charlotte kicked him on the bottom of his leg.

"Ouch," Sean said, but never stopped smiling. "You're going to pay for that."

"I look forward to it." Charlotte couldn't resist. She had to admit it felt good having Sean by her side.

# Chapter Fifty

Sean wooed the crowd with his sultry voice. The fans located near the front screamed out his name. Even with the bright lights shining in his face, Sean zoomed in on Charlotte. He kissed his two fingers and blew the kiss her way. She would know it was meant for her.

Sean walked off stage. The producer of the awards show met him backstage. "We're at commercial break now. We want you to present the next award. Do you think you can be ready when the commercial break ends?"

"Don't see why not," Sean said.

Taylor handed him a bottle of water. He took a quick gulp of it. He used the towel Taylor handed him and wiped the sweat from his forehead and off his neck and shoulders.

Taylor helped him put his suit back on.

The producer walked back over. "We need you at the podium."

"Coming," Sean responded. He buttoned his shirt and tucked it in while he walked towards the stage. "Parris, glad they paired me with you."

They hugged each other. Sean held her hand and they walked out on stage together. Everyone enjoyed the playful banter between the two of them.

"The MVA Best New Female Artist of the Year award goes to," Sean said.

Parris read the name on the hand held notebook and said, "Venus."

Sean yelled, "Congratulations, Venus."

The excited R & B singer came to the stage and accepted her award.

Sean remembered when he won his first MVA. He was so nervous that he started thanking everyone. They had to play the music on him and one of the presenters escorted him off the stage.

During the next commercial break, he went and took his seat. The producers didn't like people walking around during filming, especially at live events such as this one.

Parris and Sean won the award for best collaboration. Sean let Parris speak first. He then spoke. "I want to thank God for giving me the gift of song. To Parris for agreeing to help me out on this track. Give it up for Parris y'all." Sean clapped and the audience clapped. He went on to say. "I want to thank my sister, Marie, who couldn't be here tonight. Special shout out to my girl who's always got my back. Thanks to Team Sean, Charlotte, Jason, Felicia, Bobby, Taylor. And last, but not least, to my fans." He kissed the statue. "This one is for all of you." He held the statue in the air towards the balcony.

The fans in the balcony screamed.

He looped his arm through Parris' arm and they walked off the stage to take pictures and be interviewed by some of the entertainment reporters and bloggers.

"I don't want to miss the remainder of the show so I'll be giving interviews once the show is over," Sean said.

When the show ended, Sean led his group of people to the back of the theater. He turned to Charlotte. "I don't know how long this will take."

"I'm fine," Charlotte stated. "I see other clients here, so I'll mix and mingle."

"You are going to the Rave party with me aren't you?" Sean asked.

"Let me check with everyone else and let you know."

That wasn't the answer he was looking for. Sean walked away and went to the press booth. One of the bloggers asked, "Sean, everyone wants to know who the mystery woman is. We never see her face."

"Are you sure she exists?" Sean smiled. "Next question."

Another blogger asked, "Is it true you fired your last assistant because she was stealing from you?"

"No, that's a rumor," Sean answered. "Next."

Sean spent the next fifteen minutes answering questions. "Sorry, ladies and gentleman. I have to give time for the next person."

He waved as he saw the flash from several cameras and phone devices.

Charlotte and Parris were laughing about something. When he walked near them, they stopped. "Let me in on the joke. I want to laugh too," Sean said.

"Girl talk. You wouldn't understand." Parris winked her right eye. "There's Casper. I'll see the two of you later."

"Tell Casper, I'll be ready to record next week as promised."

"Text him later. I'm not delivering any messages."

"She's so wrong," Sean said, as he watched Parris walk away.

"You know she's going to tell him. She loves messing with you," Charlotte said.

"I get no respect."

"I respect you, honey," she teased, as she playfully hit him.

"Where's everyone else?"

"They all bailed out on us. Looks like it's just you and me."

"Let's get this party started," Sean said. He started dancing.

"Come on, silly, I'm riding with you." Charlotte walked away with Sean fast on her heels admiring the view she presented.

# Chapter Fifty-One

Charlotte and Sean went to several industry parties. They mixed and mingled and enjoyed each other's company. Charlotte stood near the bar while Sean took pictures with some of his colleagues.

"That black sure looks good on you." Charlotte recognized the voice.

Darryl was the last person she wanted to see. She stared into the face of pure evil. She turned to walk away but he grabbed her arm. She jerked it away. She took a few, deep breaths and then she turned around to face Darryl.

The party was in full swing and people were passing by. They stood closer to each other than Charlotte wanted.

"Darryl, what you're doing could be considered harassment."

Darryl laughed. "Like you harassed me all those years ago."

Charlotte had enough of feeling like a victim. "We both know that's a lie."

"You broke my heart and used me to further your career."

Charlotte felt her veins popping out of her forehead. "Stop with the lies. Your ego got deflated when I ended an engagement you really didn't want in the first place."

"It's the way you ended it. You could have come to me and let me be the one to end things."

"Are you serious? I was supposed to let you humiliate me more than you'd already done? God only knows how many women you slept with while we were together."

"I'm sorry. What more do you want me to say?" Darryl asked.

"You tried to ruin me. You made me feel like crap with your constant belittling of me. I got fired from my job because of you. Should I go on?" Charlotte now stood with her arms folded.

"Can you keep it down? People are beginning to look our way."

"If you don't leave me alone, I'm going to get even louder. I'm sure since you're now up for president of one of the largest record labels in the country, you wouldn't want a scene. Yes, Darryl, I've been keeping up with you too. So don't call me, don't email me, definitely don't stop by my office or I will tell everyone you're a bully."

"No one's going to believe you."

"The mere fact there's a possibility can ruin you. So try me if you want to." Charlotte crossed her arms.

Sean walked behind her. "Everything okay here?"

"Sean, my man. What's up?" Darryl reached out to get a handshake.

"No, man. We're not cool."

Darryl looked at Sean and then at Charlotte. "Oh, it's like that. Peace, I'm out." Darryl walked away.

"What was that all about?" Sean asked.

Charlotte took a quick gulp of her drink. "I'll tell you in the car. I'm ready to go now."

Charlotte poured herself another drink when they were inside of the limousine. Sean took the bottle from her.

"Slow down. You know what happened the last time you drank too much."

"Don't remind me."

"Did Darryl say something disrespectful to you?"

"He tried to, but I put him in his place. It felt good standing up to him too."

"Good for you," Sean responded.

"I don't have to worry about him ever again."

Sean reached for Charlotte. "Come here, baby."

Charlotte sighed and fell into his arms.

## Chapter Fifty-Two

Sean watched Charlotte as she slept. He didn't like seeing Darryl upset her. Darryl had no clue on what he was up against. Sean knew Darryl was in the running for president of his last record label. Sean vowed to make sure Darryl didn't get the position.

Charlotte reached out to him. "Baby, what are you doing over there?"

"Just thinking."

"Come and get back in the bed. It'll be time to get up before you know it," Charlotte said.

"I say we both take a long weekend. Just the two of us. We can lie in bed all day if we want to," Sean suggested.

"Okay."

Sean slipped back under the covers and lay on his back, arms crossed under his head. Charlotte lay on her side, wrapped her arms around him and placed her head on his chest. She fell back to sleep while Sean stared at the ceiling.

The sound of Sean's cell phone ringing woke them both up. Charlotte's phone started ringing too.

They both searched for their phones. Sean answered his while Charlotte answered hers. They both could be heard talking over the other.

"Say what?" Sean asked.

Sean jumped out of the bed and looked out his window. At the end of his driveway were news vans, reporters and camera operators.

"Sean, put some clothes on quick," Charlotte said.

Sean said to Taylor over the phone. "Thanks for the heads up."

Sean ended the call with Taylor and rushed to get dressed.

"Where're those clothes I left over the last time?" Charlotte asked.

"On the right side of the closet. Fresh from the cleaners."

"I wish I knew why I'm the last person to find out the police are on their way to see me," Sean said, while he got dressed.

Charlotte yelled from the closet. "There's no telling who at the LAPD is leaking this."

Charlotte's phone rang again. She came out of the closet trying to fasten her pants and talk on the phone at the same time.

Sean went to the bathroom, washed his face and brushed his teeth. He would worry about taking a shower later.

Charlotte was fully dressed in a pair of black slacks and a cream colored blouse. She'd whipped her hair up in a ponytail.

"Since the police are on their way over here with a search warrant, I called my attorney. He'll be here soon."

Sean did his best to remain calm. "If Dana was killed, I had nothing to do with it. I'm innocent. Charlotte, what am I going to do?"

"According to a police source, there's evidence here. I couldn't find out what the evidence is supposed to be."

The doorbell rang. Sean looked at Charlotte with fear in his eyes.

"I didn't have anything to do with Dana's death. You do believe me don't you?" Sean asked.

Charlotte looked Sean in the eyes. "It's not that I don't believe you. I just can't think about this on a personal level right now. I have to treat you like my client. Let me do most of the talking. The attorney will be here shortly."

This time a loud knock could be heard. Sean opened the door.

"Sean Maxwell," a uniformed officer said.

"Yes," Sean responded.

The officer handed him a piece of paper. "We have a warrant to search the premises."

Before Sean could respond, his house was bombarded with several police officers. They went from room to room searching for something that Sean was unaware of.

Charlotte held his hand. "Keep calm," she urged.

"I'm trying," he responded.

Sean watched as they went from room to room. It looked like they were going through every inch of his house.

He heard one officer say on his walkie talkie, "Everything's clear in here."

By now, a man in a suit walked in. "Charlotte, I came as soon as I could."

Charlotte walked up to the man and shook his hand. "Luke Hogan, this is my client, Sean Maxwell. He may need your representation."

Sean shook his hand. "I'm not sure of what's going on."

"Don't worry. I just need your John Hancock on this to give me the right to represent you and then I'll get to the bottom of this."

Charlotte nodded her head. He trusted her, so he signed the paper without reading it. Luke took the paper and placed it in his left pocket.

Luke said, "Let me see the search warrant and then I'll go find whoever is in charge. Relax. You're in good hands."

Sean just looked at Luke and Charlotte. Life as he knew it had ended. He stopped doing petty crimes and became a singer so he could avoid the cops in Houston and now here he was in Los Angeles being surrounded by them.

Charlotte paced back and forth outside of Sean's living room. She wished she could have been in the room with Sean and Luke when the police interrogated him. Charlotte stopped when she noticed the door opening. Luke exited but Sean remained inside. Charlotte didn't like the solemn look she saw on Luke's face.

Luke walked over to her. "It looks worse than what it is."

"So, is he being arrested?" Charlotte asked.

"That's what I'm waiting to see. I don't think they have enough evidence, but it depends on what the District Attorney wants to do at this point."

Charlotte hung her head. "I hope this new DA isn't trying to make a name for himself. If so, we're screwed. He would try him just for the notoriety."

"I've tried cases against this new DA. He's good but he's usually fair. Don't give up hope yet." Luke's phone rang. He looked down at it. "I need to take this. Wait here and I'll be back." Luke re-entered the room where Sean was.

Charlotte decided to eavesdrop. She put her ear to the door.

She heard Sean say, "The relationship I had with Dana shouldn't have bearing on your investigation. If she was killed, I want her murderer found too."

*Is he confessing that he had a relationship with her?* Charlotte asked herself.

Charlotte needed to talk to a friend. She moved away from the door and called Mona. She'd given Mona an update. "Mona, I don't know what to believe. It sounded like there was more to his relationship than he'd told me." She turned around and to her surprise Sean and Luke were standing nearby. "I have to go. I'll call you later."

Charlotte rushed over to Sean. "Are you okay? Are they through with their investigation?"

"They want me to come down to the police station for further questioning," Sean said in a dry voice.

"I'll go get the car and meet you both out front," Luke said.

Luke left them alone.

"I think it's best Luke and I handle this alone."

"But you need me to mediate between you and the press. Trust me. This is a delicate situation and I would never leave you out there to fend for yourself."

"You're getting paid a hefty twenty percent so I'm going to let you do your job with the press, but I don't need you to be there."

Charlotte opened her mouth to say something but didn't. She would forgive him for his snide remark.

"I've called Jason. He's just waiting on me to call him back. He's already drafting a release to send out."

"Charlotte, no disrespect, but I really don't feel like talking right now."

"You don't have to talk. Just know that I'm taking care of everything."

Charlotte and Sean walked to the front door and opened it. She could see

Luke's car and a crowd of reporters at the end of the driveway.

Charlotte tried to comfort Sean by holding his hand but he moved his hand away.

Sean turned to Charlotte. "Since you don't trust me, I don't need you at the police station with me."

"What are you talking about, Sean? I'm here for you." Sean gave her a skeptical look. Had he overheard her conversation with Mona?

"Luke's waiting on me and I really don't have time to go back and forth with you. I'll keep Jason and Taylor posted on what's going on with me. You can go and deal with your other *clients*."

Sean, with his head held low, left Charlotte standing in the doorway of his house as he entered Luke's car.

# Chapter Fifty-Three

Later on that day, Charlotte tried to contact Sean to find out what happened at the police station but he wasn't returning her calls. She replayed their last conversation over and over in her head. She should have cleared up what he'd overheard her say to Mona.

Yes, for a moment she was questioning whether or not he'd ever slept with Dana, but she never believed he'd had anything to do with her death. As she thought more and more about it, she knew in her heart Sean was telling the truth about him and Dana not having an intimate relationship.

If he would take her calls, she could tell him that, but he wouldn't. She felt miserable. She curled up on the couch and called Kem. Kem put her on hold and got Mona on the line with them.

"I feel like I let him down," Charlotte fretted. "He's having to deal with this by himself. I should be there with him now."

"Calm down," Kem said. "He won't take your calls so just go over there."

"I can't just pop up at his house uninvited," Charlotte sighed.

"You're his manager. He's going through a crisis. You don't need his permission," Mona said.

"Charlotte, it's clear to me it's all just one big understanding. So all you have to do is go over there and let Sean know that. Use the excuse that you're there strictly on business," Kem suggested.

"Kem and I agree, so get your behind off the couch and go make things right with your man," Mona said.

"I don't know what to believe," repeated itself over and over in Sean's head. Hearing her speak those words cut him deep. Seeing the pain in her eyes didn't help matters or maybe the pain was actually doubt. She must doubt his innocence or she never would have said it to her friend, Mona.

Sean stayed in the shower so long the water turned cold. He turned the knob and got out of the tub. He dried off hoping that the police found a resolution to Dana's murder. He wasn't guilty of any crimes and he didn't want the cloud of doubt hanging over his head.

He heard a knock.

"I'll be out in a minute," Sean said.

Sean removed a black terry cloth robe from the wall and placed it on. He tied the robe tight. He opened the door and Charlotte was standing near the foot of his bed.

"What are you doing here?" Sean asked.

"I'm here to check on you," Charlotte stated.

"Where's Taylor?" Sean looked away and asked.

"He's down stairs. He's the one who let me in," Charlotte replied.

"Send him up. I need to talk to him about some things," Sean said. He went to his closet to find something to put on.

He picked a pair of jeans and a t-shirt. He picked out a pair of sneakers to match his shirt.

Charlotte stood in the same place where he left her.

"What? I thought I asked you to send Taylor up," Sean inquired, as he went to put on his clothes.

"I'm on your side, remember?"

Sean looked at Charlotte. "Really? Are you really on my side? Or are you just here to earn your paycheck?"

Charlotte placed one hand on her hip. "Your current circumstances do not give you the right to talk to me any kind of way."

"You're right. I apologize. I shouldn't mix my personal feelings with business." Sean sat on the bed and put on his sneakers.

"What happened in the interrogation room?" Charlotte asked. She now stood near him.

"Nothing I want to talk about." He tied up his shoes without looking at her.

Charlotte reached for him. Sean leaned back.

"Don't act like you care," Sean said.

Charlotte grabbed Sean's hand. This time he didn't pull away. "Sean, all of this has been one big misunderstanding. I know you overheard my conversation with Mona. I should have cleared things up immediately but I didn't so I'm here to do so now. I'm sorry if it came across as me not trusting you."

"I felt like you were abandoning me at a crucial time," Sean said.

"I overheard what you told the detective. I was just talking the situation through." She patted her heart with her free hand. "I know in my heart you're innocent of everything people are trying to accuse you of."

"Looks like I have a lot to think about," Sean responded.

"Take all the time you need. I'll send Taylor right up." Charlotte released his hand and left him alone with his thoughts.

Sean felt a sigh of relief after Charlotte cleared up the misunderstanding. In order to get through this ordeal, he needed her to believe in him.

A few minutes later, Taylor stood in his doorway. Taylor exclaimed, "The phone won't stop ringing. The voicemail is full. I can't respond to the emails fast enough."

"Slow down," Sean said. "As soon as Charlotte's people finish the press release, I want you to post it to my page. You don't have to address those emails one by one. In fact, delete them. Don't even bother to read the negativity."

Sean and Taylor went downstairs where Charlotte and Jason were both on their phones and iPads doing things.

Jason said, "Sean, I'm with you so don't stress out."

"Thanks, man," Sean responded.

Charlotte placed her hand over her cell phone. "We got this handled. Taylor, can you check to see what's wrong with the printer?"

"Yes, ma'am," Taylor responded. Taylor went straight to the printer and began troubleshooting.

Sean watched Charlotte and wondered why he even doubted her. She'd proven herself time and time again. With Charlotte by his side, he would be able to face anything.

Taylor got the printer working. The printer shot out several pages. Jason picked up a sheet, scanned it and walked over to Sean and handed it to him.

"How does this sound?" Jason asked.

Sean read the press release emphasizing his innocence. "Sounds good to me."

"Taylor, what's your email address?" Jason asked.

Jason and Taylor went to the desk and talked.

Sean stepped over to the couch and sat next to Charlotte. He waited for her to get off the phone. "I want to apologize for how I acted earlier," Sean said.

"Forgiven. I know you're under a lot of stress," Charlotte replied. Her hands never left her phone. He noticed her texting.

"No excuses. I thought you doubted me and that hurt."

Charlotte placed her phone down in her lap and looked up at him. "Sean, if I doubted you, I wouldn't be here right now. I wouldn't be doing my best to make sure this incident didn't get blown out of proportion."

"You say that, but it's your job. You would be doing it anyway."

"But would I be doing this?"

Charlotte got up and kissed him. She'd never kissed him in front of anyone. Although Jason knew something was going on between the two of them, she'd never confirmed it.

Her public display of affection caught Sean off-guard. She pulled back and took her seat. "Any more doubts?" she asked.

"None," he responded, as he licked his lips.

# Chapter Fifty-Four

Sean and Taylor left Charlotte and Jason alone in the office. Charlotte responded to a few emails about Sean's situation by providing the link to the press release Jason sent out. She stopped and looked out into open space thinking about the kiss. She'd gotten caught up in the moment. She wanted to erase Sean's doubts. At the time, she'd forgotten that Jason and Taylor were in the room.

Jason got off the phone and walked over to the desk and stood in front of Charlotte. "I knew something was going on between the two of you."

"So who are you now, the love guru?" Charlotte laughed.

"That's one of my many talents." Jason laughed.

Sean walked in the room. "I'm glad someone's found something to laugh about."

Charlotte turned towards Sean. "Team Sean is working on this. You'll have reasons to smile again soon."

Charlotte's phone rang. "This is Charlotte," she answered.

"I'm outside. Someone let me in," Luke said. "I'm not alone. Detective Watkins is with me."

Charlotte looked at Jason. "Go let Luke and the detective in."

Charlotte turned her attention back to the phone. "Someone's coming now."

Sean's forehead crunched up. Charlotte could tell he was stressed. She walked over to him and squeezed his hand. "It's going to be alright. Have I ever let you down?" she asked.

He shook his head no. "I try to do right so why is this happening to me?"

"I wish I had the answers. But I think Luke and the detective might."

She released Sean's hand just as Luke, the detective and Jason entered the room.

"Have a seat," Charlotte said.

Charlotte sat at the end of the couch next to Sean. Jason stood behind them.

"I'll let Detective Watkins tell you what we've discovered," Luke said.

The redheaded Detective had a slight slur when he spoke. "Luke brought to my attention that our source used to be your personal assistant. Do you know a Priscilla Franklin?"

Sean responded, "Yes. He's correct. She was my assistant."

"He fired her," Charlotte added.

"We think Priscilla killed Dana and tried to make it look like a suicide," Detective Watkins said.

"Are you sure you're talking about the Priscilla I know?" Sean rubbed his head.

"There's no doubt, Mr. Maxwell."

Sean opened his mouth to say something but closed it. He finally said, "I'm just shocked."

"It may come as a surprise, but it's been my experience that most victims are killed by someone they know. Did Dana and Priscilla get along?" Detective Watkins asked.

"Yes. As far as I know. They were always laughing and joking with one another. Dana would sometimes take Priscilla on shopping sprees," Sean responded.

"Even if she did it, why try to set up Sean?" Charlotte asked.

"You've confirmed she was fired. Apparently Sean firing her, set off another chain of emotions for her."

"So I've been questioned and ridiculed in the media, all because of some false accusations?"

"We know that now and I would like to apologize for any inconvenience we've caused you. I know the media can be a hound when they sniff a story out; especially one involving someone of your statue," Detective Watkins said.

"Is she in custody is all I want to know," Charlotte blurted out.

"Ms. Franklin hasn't been brought in yet. This is where we hoped you could come in." Detective Watkins looked at Sean. "Our case would be air tight if we could get a confession."

Sean threw his hand up in the air. "I'm out of this. You'll have to find another way."

"Sean, I think it's in your best interest to cooperate. She can always say you asked her to do it. We need her confession to protect you," Luke added.

"He's right. Call her," Charlotte said.

Sean pulled out his phone and called Priscilla. "Priscilla, I need to talk to you. I'm sorry for how I acted. Can you stop by the house?"

Sean hit the speaker button. Priscilla responded, "I knew you would come running to me."

"Can you come by the house or not?" Sean asked.

"I'll be there in an hour. Don't worry about a thing. I'll fix this mess you seem to have gotten yourself into."

Priscilla disconnected the call.

Detective Watkins said, "An hour doesn't give us much time to set up but we'll have to make it work."

"I have security cameras in place. I just need to get the sound activated."

"Show me where the device is and I will figure out a way to activate it," Detective Watkins said.

Sean got up. "Follow me."

Charlotte said to Luke. "Thank you. Sean means a lot to me and without your help, I'm not sure if he would be walking around a free man or in jail for something he didn't do."

"Lucky for you, my dear, he won't ever have to find out," Luke patted her hand and left the room.

Charlotte said to Jason, "Let's get rid of our stuff. I think this is the best place for him to bring her for their conversation. Plus, there's a door right over there where we can hide and listen."

"I'm not going to ask you how you know this," Jason said.

"I'm observant. Watch and learn, young man. Watch and learn." Charlotte smiled, as her and Jason cleaned up the office area.

# Chapter Fifty-Five

Sean tested out the camera angle and sound for Detective Watkins. He called him on his cell phone to let him know everything was working. Luke remained in the security closet with the detective. Charlotte, Jason and Taylor were in the nearby room.

He'd moved his cars out of the garage so they could hide their cars there. Sean heard the doorbell. He still couldn't believe Priscilla was capable of something like this and part of him hoped they were wrong about her. Either way, Sean needed to put on the performance of his life because his freedom was on the line.

He opened the door. Priscilla, wearing a skin-tight mini-dress, walked in and hugged him. "I've missed you," she squealed.

Sean said, "I've missed you too. That's why I asked you over here."

"Where's your new assistant?" Priscilla asked.

"He had to go," Sean responded.

"What did he do?" she asked.

"Come to my office. We can talk there," Sean responded.

Sean made sure they were in clear view of the cameras.

Priscilla stood near him. "I'm glad you called me. I needed to see you," Priscilla said.

Sean looked down at her. "I'm going to be honest. Things haven't been the same since I let you go."

"Does that mean you want me back?" Priscilla's eyes widened.

"I couldn't ask you to come back and work for me."

Priscilla got closer to him, but he stepped back. The camera needed to get a clear view of her face.

"If you were to ask, I would come back," she said.

"I need to be able to trust my assistant." Sean went and sat behind his desk.

"You can trust me. I'm the one who has always had your back." Priscilla walked and stood in front of the desk.

"I'm dealing with so much right now. You've seen the reports. You know they suspect me of doing something to Dana."

"You didn't kill Dana. I know that and if you hire me back, I will make sure they know it too," Priscilla said.

Sean leaned forward. "How are you going to do that? I have a defense attorney and Charlotte working on this. They haven't been able to help me so far."

Priscilla walked around the desk and sat on the edge. "That's just it. You're always falling for the wrong women. When you've got the right package standing in front of you. I'm all the woman you'll ever need. You didn't need Dana and you sure in the hell don't need Charlotte."

"There was never anything going on between me and Dana," Sean said.

"I know, but Dana wanted something to happen. I'm just glad you didn't fall for her tricks. Too bad you caught feelings for Charlotte, though," Priscilla sputtered.

"Let's not talk about Charlotte." Sean looked away.

Priscilla placed her hand on his face. He turned and looked at her. Priscilla asked, "Did she hurt you like I knew she would?"

"Yes. But I'll be all right. You're here with me now. Things will be just fine." Sean gazed into Priscilla's eyes.

"Sean, don't worry. I'm going to get rid of her just like I got rid of Dana. Charlotte will never hurt another man."

Sean grabbed Dana by the wrist. "What do you mean, 'just like you got rid of Dana?' Priscilla, what did you do?"

Priscilla stood and jerked her wrist out of Sean's grasp. "Dana's consistent

*221*

harassing was stressing you out. I couldn't have you upset so I went to visit her. I pretended like you'd sent me. I gave her a bottle of wine and a box of chocolate with a card signed by you. I'd already laced the wine with medicine identical to what she'd been prescribed. She thought I was celebrating with her but I was only there to make sure the overdose of pills mixed with the wine worked. I waited hours for her to fade into death."

"I don't know what to say." Sean couldn't stand to look at Priscilla. He couldn't believe she'd murdered Dana to be with him. What did that mean for Charlotte?

Priscilla walked closer to him. "Thank me by giving me my job back. I can get rid of Charlotte too. Just say the word."

Sean had a puzzled look on his face. "Priscilla, you amaze me."

Priscilla rambled on. "And you know what's so beautiful about the whole thing? I went through Dana's stuff and found a letter. Apparently, she'd been thinking about suicide. So, in a way, I was helping Dana do something she wanted to do herself."

Sean stood. He now towered over Priscilla. His anger rose. "Are you the source that the police say tipped them on to me?"

"I...I...I would never betray you," Priscilla stuttered.

"You're the only person who had a reason to. What you did could have ruined me. What were you thinking?" Sean slammed his fist down on the desk beside Priscilla.

"I knew you'd hire a good attorney."

"You were counting on me to get out of this, but what if I hadn't? What if I had been sent to prison for a crime I didn't commit? Would you have confessed?" Sean blurted out. Veins in Sean's forehead were visible.

Priscilla body shook with fear. "Sean, I'm sorry."

Sean got down in Priscilla's face. He clenched his fist. He'd never hit a woman before but at that moment in time, he wanted to.

Charlotte rushed inside and grabbed his arm. "Sean, don't."

"What is she doing here?" Priscilla said, after being caught off-guard.

Detective Watkins and Luke entered the room. Detective Watkins held out a pair of handcuffs, "Priscilla Franklin, you are under arrest for the murder of Dana Reliford." His voice trailed off

"Sean, I can't believe you. You set me up. You set me up to be with *that*." She pointed at Charlotte.

Detective Watkins grabbed Priscilla's arm and pushed it behind her back. There was a slight struggle, but he was able to get the handcuffs on. He continued to recite the Miranda rights to her.

"This isn't over," Priscilla shouted as she was being led out the house by Detective Watkins.

"Well done. They got enough evidence to convict her," Luke explained. He patted Sean on the back. "Looks like my job is done here. Good day." He tipped his hat and left.

"If I could tell someone, they would never believe it," Taylor said.

Jason wrapped his arm around Taylor's shoulder. "But you're going to keep what happened here to yourself right?"

"Yes," Taylor said.

"Just checking. Why don't you and I make ourselves scarce so these two can talk," Jason insisted.

Sean looked at Charlotte and without saying a word, she walked over to him and wrapped her arms around his waist. "You all right?" she asked.

He squeezed her tight. "I am now."

# Chapter Fifty-Six

*Sean Maxwell's Assistant Accused of Murdering His Ex-Manager* was the headline that flooded the internet. With Charlotte's advice, Sean was able to get through another crisis.

Charlotte placed her iPad on the coffee table and curled up with Sean on his couch. It'd been forty-eight hours since Priscilla's confession. Between the phone calls, the interviews, they both were exhausted. "I don't think I can make it up the stairs."

"Neither can I. I vote we sleep right here."

Charlotte lay back on Sean's chest and closed her eyes.

Neither woke up from that position until the next day.

Charlotte woke up first. She saw Taylor hovering over them.

"Taylor, warn somebody the next time," Charlotte said, as her body shook.

Sean's eyes popped open. "What's going on?"

Charlotte sat up. "It's just Taylor."

"I was trying to wake Sean. You have an interview with E Hollywood. Their crew should be here any minute."

"Oh my goodness. And I look a hot mess," Charlotte said.

"Calm down, baby. It's me they are coming to see." Sean yawned and then stood.

Sean said to Taylor. "Stall them if they get here before I come back downstairs."

"Will do," Taylor responded.

Charlotte and Sean went upstairs to Sean's room. "I'll use the guest bath,"

Charlotte said, as she removed her underwear from out of her overnight bag.

Sean wrapped his arm around her waist. "I need you to wash my back so you're coming with me."

"Go on, Sean, you don't have much time."

Sean picked her up from behind and her feet were now dangling. He started walking towards the bathroom. "I know, so let's get this shower started."

"Sean, stop. You're going to make us both fall," she said, laughing uncontrollably.

Charlotte didn't protest any more. Sean put her down once they were inside of the bathroom.

They undressed and got in the shower. Sean turned around to face her. The water slid down his back. The steam from the hot water fogged up the mirrors. "I never thanked you properly," Sean said, as he got down on his knees, placed his hands between her thighs and opened her legs.

"We don't have time," Charlotte mumbled, but changed her tune when his lips found her center. Within seconds, Charlotte's protest turned to moans of pleasure.

She held on to the shower walls and climaxed into Sean's mouth. Sean stood revealing his stiff manhood.

Sean brought his mouth on top of hers and devoured it. She leaned back on the wall of the shower. Sean positioned one of her legs around his waist and slid inside of her wet walls.

Charlotte gasped with pleasure.

"I love you, Sean," Charlotte moaned as their united bodies danced to a euphoric rhythm.

"I love you too," Sean said, as he held Charlotte and released his seed inside of her.

An hour later, they were both dressed and downstairs greeting the crew and entertainment reporter, Freda.

Charlotte stood on the sidelines as the crew filmed Sean in different areas of his house. Freda's questions were light but Charlotte knew eventually she would get around to asking Sean about Dana and Priscilla.

"I would like to finish the segment with me asking you a few questions from your living room."

"Sure. After you," Sean said.

Charlotte stood behind one of the camera operators while he tested the lighting and camera angles. He said, "Ready, when you are, Freda."

Freda ran her hand through the back of her natural hair. "How do I look?"

"You're shining," the make-up artist said. She walked up to her and used a matte sponge with powder. "Now you're perfect."

"On three," the camera operator instructed. He held up three fingers and counted down.

Freda looked in the camera and then at Sean. "We're back with Sean Maxwell. He's opened up his home to us. He's shared with us some of his struggles. We were all shocked when we learned about what happened earlier this week. Sean, how are you dealing with all of this?"

Sean responded, "Prayer for one. I have a good support system." He looked in Charlotte's direction. "My fans have been wonderful."

Charlotte watched as Sean talked about his feelings and now his personal cause.

Freda asked, "I know we were just talking about something very serious, but there's a question your fans are dying to know the answer to and I promised I would ask and then we'll end our segment."

"Go for it."

"Who is this mystery woman you're always posting about? Can I get an exclusive, please," Freda smiled.

Sean smiled in Charlotte's direction but it appeared as if he was looking into the camera.

"I'm not sure if she's ready for the world to know who she is just yet. I can say that she's special to me. She's captured my heart with her love and kindness. I trust her with my life. There's no other woman like her. She's my rock."

Freda was on the edge of her seat. "You sound so in love. I hope she's watching."

"I'm sure she is," Sean responded.

Freda looked into the camera and smiled. "Maybe when Sean's mystery woman feels like revealing herself, he'll give us the exclusive. This is Freda with E Entertainment and we're all about love."

Freda removed her microphone. She turned to Sean and said, "Good interview. I mean it. When you're ready to go public, call me."

Freda and her crew left. Charlotte picked up her keys and purse. "I must be going myself. I'll see you later."

"Are you going to the Laker's game with me?"

"I'm kind of tired. Why don't you just drop by afterwards," Charlotte said.

Sean walked Charlotte to the front door. He kissed her and then watched her leave. He waited until she pulled away before closing the door.

Kem and Mona stood near one of the stands at center court of the Staples Center next to Charlotte. They watched Sean sing the Star-Spangled Banner. He hit each note with precision. The whole stadium cheered when he sang the last stanza.

The announcer said over the intercom. "Sean Maxwell, don't leave the floor yet."

Sean turned around with a puzzled look on his face.

Kem and Mona gave Charlotte a slight nudge. "Go on," Kem said.

Charlotte took a few deep breaths and walked towards Sean. She ignored the stares from the crowd in the sold-out arena.

The announcer handed Charlotte the microphone. "I'm breaking one of my own rules but needed to let you know here and now, that I love you."

Sean leaned close to Charlotte. "You do realize we're in front of thousands of people and this is being televised, right?" Sean asked, a smile never leaving his face.

Charlotte loved Sean and didn't care who knew. She was ready to give him the type of commitment he wanted from her. "I want the world to know how much you mean to me." Charlotte reached for Sean's hand and held it.

Sean grabbed the microphone from Charlotte. He dropped down on one knee.

Charlotte looked down into his eyes and asked, "What are you doing?"

Sean sang, *"Charlotte, will you marry me?"*

A hush fell over the stadium as they all waited on Charlotte's response.

"Yes. Yes, Sean, I'll marry you," Charlotte responded.

Sean stood, embraced Charlotte and their lips locked. It became the kiss seen around the world.

# About the Author

Shelia M. Goss is a screenwriter and the *Essence* magazine and *Dallas Morning News* bestselling author of over eighteen novels, including *The Bad Twin, Star Struck, V.I.P., Her Invisible Husband, The Commitment Plan, The Joneses, etc.* Shelia has received many accolades for her books over the years, including being a 2012 and 2014 Emma Awards Finalist for two of her romance novels. *Library Journal* named *The Joneses* as one of the best books of 2014. A speaker at literary conferences across the country, Shelia also works closely with librarians supporting literacy and increasing awareness via workshops for adults and teens.

You can learn more about Shelia at: www.sheliagoss.com
Facebook: www.facebook.com/shelia.goss
Twitter: @sheliamgoss

*He thought he would teach her a lesson but he's about to get schooled.*

## How to Avoid a Billionaire
© 2015 Tressie Lockwood

Ryder Neyland grew up immersed in the cutthroat world of million-dollar deals. From his father's CEO friends, he learned how to handle people and money, and quickly learned rule number one: never allow anyone to cross him without retribution.

When he learns the identity of a small-time ad exec who masterminded the advertisement that not only cost him millions of dollars, but made him look like a corporate bully, he sets out to put the woman in her place.

Melanie Cai is ecstatic when, for once, her boss gives her full credit for the campaign she hopes will launch her career. Which makes it all the more intriguing when Ryder begins seducing her in a decidedly non-gourmet diner, apparently thinking she doesn't recognize him. He's sexy. She's tempted. Why not play along?

It isn't long before Ryder's plan for revenge starts running off the rails. Melanie may have killer curves, but she doesn't easily bend to his manipulations. And soon she has him not only rethinking his world view, but also his future.

*Warning: Contains a high-powered executive who isn't used to hearing "no", and a half African-American, half Chinese ad exec who knows her place—and it ain't under his thumb. Unless that thumb is right where she wants it…*

# SAMHAIN
PUBLISHING

*It's all about the story...*

## Romance

## HORROR

## Retro ROMANCE

www.samhainpublishing.com

DISCARD/SOLD
FRIENDS MLS